Undisclosed

NIGHTS SERIES BOOK SEVEN

A.M. SALINGER

COPYRIGHT

Undisclosed (Nights Series Book 7)
Copyright © 2018 by A.M. Salinger
All rights reserved.
Registered with the US Copyright Office.
Second paperback edition: 2024
ISBN: 978-1-9996184-6-9

www.AMSalinger.com
shop.adstarrling.com

Edited by www.ElfwerksEditing.com
Cover Design by A.M. Salinger

BOOKS BY A.M. SALINGER

NIGHTS

One Night - 1

The Escort - 2

Tokyo Heat - 3

Sweet Obsession - 4

Sweet Possession - 5

The Proposition - 6

Undisclosed - 7

Hush - 8

One Day - 9

Nights Series Short Story Collection

TWILIGHT FALLS

Alex - 1

Carter - 2

Hunter - 3

Wyatt - 4

Drake - 5

Tristan - 6

Miles - 7

Urban Fantasy Romance written as

Ava Marie Salinger

Fallen Messengers

Fractured Souls - 1

Spellbound - 2

Edge Lines - 3

Oathbreaker - 4

Harbinger - 5

Crimson Skies - 6

Wicked - Fallen Messengers Short Story Collection

CHAPTER ONE

Eveline Claude blinked slowly. "Come again?"

A muscle jumped in the jawline of the man seated on the other side of the conference room table.

"You don't own the freehold to the Tokyo branch of *Le Secret*," Malcolm Brooks repeated stiffly.

Eveline's pulse started to race as she stared from Brooks to his poker-faced partner, Victor Kline.

"I'm sorry, did I just hear you say that I don't own the tenure of one of my most successful business enterprises?" Silence greeted her stunned question. "Are you guys yanking my chain right now?" Eveline chuckled in disbelief. "You are, aren't you? Because there's no way my one-thousand-dollar-per-hour, top-notch city lawyers just informed me that they fucked up."

Brooks glanced at Kline. "Told you she'd bring up the hourly fee," he muttered.

Kline ignored his partner and studied Eveline with

an impassive expression. "Of course, we'll be working to resolve this matter pro bono. The mistake is ours and we cannot apologize enough on behalf of the firm."

Eveline's mouth went dry as she looked between the two men and realized they were serious. The first inkling that her day was going to turn out to be gloriously shitty began at six a.m., when the fire alarm in her apartment building went off. Having left *Le Secret* at two, Eveline wasn't pleased that her much needed beauty sleep had been interrupted by some asshole who hadn't figured out how to use his new waffle maker. Her ire rose tenfold when she went to collect her car from the underground garage and noticed the fresh scratch on her midnight blue Maserati. She'd made a note to ask the security guards to check the cameras covering the parking lot and had barreled out of the building and into the early morning Tokyo traffic at twice the allowed speed limit; she hated being late for an appointment and her nine o'clock meeting with Brooks & Kline was taking place on the other side of town. She'd made it to their office on the twelfth floor of the glass and steel high-rise housing their law firm with four minutes to spare and had waited impatiently in the conference room, curious as to why they'd requested the urgent face to face.

It was Brooks who'd called her the day before to set up the meeting.

"Something's come up. We need to talk," the lawyer said cryptically after Eveline's assistant put his call through.

Eveline paused and lowered her cup of coffee, her gaze shifting from the busy dual computer screens on the desk before her, to the glorious views beyond the panoramic windows to her right. Her office was located next to a small, private flat she kept above Le Secret and overlooked Ginza, the most famous and exclusive district in Tokyo.

Eveline frowned as she studied the busy intersection outside, the first seed of unease stirring inside her.

"What's this about, Malcolm? It's rare for you to call me yourself."

"I know. It would be best if we had this conversation face to face," Brooks replied.

He'd refused to answer Eveline's questions and gave her the details of their appointment before disconnecting. Though she'd been troubled by her enigmatic conversation with the lawyer, Eveline soon forgot about the exchange, the daily demands of running her internationally renowned and incredibly successful chain of upscale escort clubs consuming all her attention and focus. Business was booming, especially since she'd opened the latest branch of *Le Secret* in Singapore.

Eveline swallowed presently and leaned back in the sleek metal and leather chair of the conference room, her knuckles whitening where she gripped the arm rests. *Maybe I should have thrown salt over my left shoulder before I left my apartment this morning. Or burned some incense or do whatever it is people do to ward off bad luck.*

She studied the two lawyers with narrowed eyes. "Explain to me exactly how this happened."

Brooks sighed and pinched the bridge of his nose while Kline slid a file across the table.

"It seems Mr. Nagato forged the documents his lawyers provided to us five years ago, when he sold you the plot in Ginza as a freehold," Brooks said bitterly. "What you actually bought off him was the right to lease. His son-in-law works for the local land registry office and we suspect he made the counterfeit papers. According to one of our contacts in the Tokyo Metropolitan Police Department, the Nagatos have connections with an organized crime syndicate that specializes in land rights grabs."

Eveline tensed, her gaze skimming the folder before her distractedly. "You mean, they're part of the Yakuza?"

Kline grimaced. "They are linked to them in a distant, convoluted fashion, yes."

Eveline's heart pounded as she digested the implication of the lawyers' words. The Yakuza were the Japanese equivalent of the Italian Mafia. Having witnessed secondhand what the mob did to their business rivals in New York, Eveline had no desire to associate with the local criminal organizations here in Japan, even if she suspected several of the clients who had visited the Tokyo branch of *Le Secret* over the last five years had some kind of connection to them.

Eveline clenched her jaw. "What can we do about this? I paid Nagato a hefty sum of money for that land. We're talking seven figures here, as you both well know." She paused, an unwelcome thought bringing a bitter taste to her mouth. "Wait. Did he even *own* that plot? Don't tell me the asshole sold me someone else's—"

"He does," Kline said. "Or he did."

"We've already lodged an appeal in court to contest the new owner's claim to the freehold," Brooks said. He ran a hand through his hair. "It's going to take some time to—"

"New owner?" Eveline scowled. "What the hell do you mean, *new owner?*" She jumped to her feet and leaned her hands on the table. "Are you telling me that conniving bastard sold *my* land to someone else?!"

"Yes," Brooks said quietly. "And this time, the documents he provided were the legitimate ones."

Eveline took a shuddering breath and closed her eyes briefly, her nails biting into her palms where she'd fisted her fingers.

"I'm gonna kill him," she hissed. Eveline grabbed her bag and stormed toward the conference room exit. "I'm gonna strangle that lowlife with my bare hands and dump his body in Tokyo Bay! What's his address?"

"Sit down, Eveline," Kline said with a sigh.

Eveline stopped by the door and whirled around. "I'm not kidding, Victor! I hope you guys know a good criminal lawyer 'cause I'm going to need—"

"Nagato is dead," Brooks said.

Eveline froze. She opened and closed her mouth soundlessly, her eyes rounding as she gaped at the two lawyers.

"*What?!*" she shrieked.

"Nagato died three weeks ago," Kline stated. "It was a heart attack, apparently."

A light-headed feeling swept over Eveline. She made her way back to the table on unsteady legs and flopped down in the chair she had just vacated.

"He completed the sale of the freehold a few days before his death," Brooks added.

Kline leaned across the table and opened the file in front of Eveline. "This is the letter we received yesterday from the new owner's law firm."

Eveline blinked before focusing on the top sheet of the paperwork before her.

"The land in Ginza is now the property of Lincoln Hudson, the President and CEO of the Hudson Group," Kline continued. "His lawyers have given us formal notice that *Le Secret*'s leasehold rights will be revoked in thirty days."

Eveline's hands trembled as she picked up the letter and read it over, the words blurring in front of her eyes. Her heart sank as she finally absorbed its content.

It was just as Kline had said.

The new owner of the plot on which *Le Secret* stood had given her thirty days to dissolve her business and vacate his land.

"Wouldn't a leasehold be for fifty years?" Eveline mumbled. "Can he even do this?"

"The new leasehold law that came into effect twenty-five years ago gives the landowner the right to refuse the leaseholder permission to run a business on his property," Kline said. "Hudson is completely within his rights to issue a revocation order."

Blood thundered in Eveline's ears, the sound matching the emotions storming through her as she stared blindly at the printed text. She put the letter down, inhaled shakily, and stared at the men opposite her.

When it rains, it fucking pours.

"How long will the court appeal take?" she said, her voice growing steely as cogwheels started turning in her brain. She had not come this far in life without learning how to roll with some punches. Eveline frowned. *Or how to get back up and knock the enemy right out of the ring.*

"Six weeks," Brooks said.

Eveline drummed the fingers of her right hand on the table, her polished, red-lacquered nails rapping an impatient tempo.

"Can we do anything to expedite it?"

"We've got a meeting with one of the judges this afternoon," Kline said. "As to whether he will be willing to bring the case forward is not something I'd want to bet money on."

Eveline gritted her teeth. "Do the Hudson Group President and his lawyers know the details of this affair? As in Nagato swindling me out of—"

"They know," Brooks said. "We spoke to Lincoln Hudson's lawyers and his secretary yesterday after we received the letter. Hudson's secretary got back to us thirty minutes ago."

Eveline leaned forward in her chair, her heart pounding against her ribs. "And? Is he willing to negotiate something?"

"Hudson said that it ain't his problem," Kline muttered.

Eveline stilled. "What?"

Brooks rubbed his eyes tiredly. "According to his secretary, Lincoln Hudson's exact words were 'I don't give a flying fuck'."

CHAPTER TWO

"I WOULD RATHER STAB MYSELF IN THE EYE WITH A pitchfork," Lincoln Hudson groaned into his cell phone.

A bark of female laughter echoed from the other end of the line.

"Seriously, Linc," his sister Julia berated in an amused voice, "it's just a charity ball. You probably won't even see them if you come early. You know what they're like for putting on a late show."

Lincoln sighed and dragged a hand down his face. "I've done my damnedest to make sure the Hudson Group isn't linked to any of his campaigns since I started the business, and I'm sure as hell not about to change that habit now."

A weary silence filled the connection.

"I know how you feel about being even remotely associated with him, Linc," Julia said quietly. "Trust me, I do. If it wasn't for Adam's job, I wouldn't be in his social circle either." She paused. "But nothing you do will ever change the fact that you're his son. Or that he's a U.S. senator."

Lincoln clamped his jaw shut to stop the automatic outburst threatening to erupt from him. Even though it had been twelve years since he'd last spoken to his father, he could still recall the rage he'd felt that day and the ugly words they'd exchanged.

As far as Lincoln was concerned, his relationship with Harry Hudson ended the day Lincoln and Julia's mother Madeleine died in a tragic car accident, a month before Lincoln turned twenty-five. Although the police report stated Madeleine Hudson had lost control of her vehicle while traveling at twice the speed limit, Lincoln knew it was news of Harry Hudson's latest affair that had caused her to get behind the wheel that night.

Everyone in the Hudson household was aware of Harry Hudson's long history of infidelity, including the servants and even the Hudsons' closest friends. Lincoln was fifteen when he first discovered his father's adultery, after he walked in on the senator with his hand up the new maid's skirt in the kitchen pantry. Although the man mumbled something about losing a personal item and stumbled past Lincoln on his way out of the room, all it took was one look at the maid's flushed face and the terror in her eyes for Lincoln to understand exactly what his father had been doing.

From that day forth, Lincoln lost all respect for the man who had sired him and could only grit his teeth in the decade that followed as he watched his father bed conquest after conquest. His so-called friends eagerly fed him the details of the senator's extramarital affairs even after he went to Yale to do his business degree.

Like nearly everyone he and his sister had associated with since their high school days, Lincoln knew the men and women who hung around him at college did so because of who his father was. There were only a handful of people he and Julia could call true friends, even now.

But it wasn't someone from Lincoln's fake entourage who brought him news of Harry Hudson's most recent affair on the day Madeleine Hudson died. Instead, it was one of Madeleine's closest friends who happened to have been a bridesmaid in Madeleine and Harry's wedding and was the mother of Madeleine's only goddaughter. She'd stormed into the Hudson family mansion during the week that Lincoln had come home for fall recess and screamed at Madeleine at the top of her head that she was a failure as a woman for not satisfying Harry in bed.

Because this time, Harry Hudson had done the truly unforgivable. Not only had he slept with the daughter of Madeleine's friend, a girl thirty years his junior, he'd gotten her pregnant and forced her to have an abortion.

Even though Lincoln knew Harry Hudson was not directly responsible for the death of his and Julia's mother, he might as well have been the one who caused the accident that took her life. True to form, Harry Hudson had used his wife's death to garner support for his political campaigns and remarried eighteen months later, this time to a woman barely older than Lincoln.

That was the final twist of the knife which had forever severed Lincoln's connection with his father.

"So, what do you say, Linc?" Julia said, bringing him back to the present. "It's a cause close to your heart. Besides, it's in Honolulu, just a skip and a hop from where you are right now."

Lincoln smiled wryly. Trust his sister to call four thousand miles of open sea a skip and a hop.

"Let me think about it," he muttered.

"So, that's a yes?" Julia said excitedly.

"That's a maybe, Flame Foot," Lincoln said tersely.

Julia muttered something rude at her old nickname. She'd hated her protruding second toes with a passion since she turned ten.

"Talk to you later, Monster Meat," she retorted.

Lincoln grinned at his own nickname from his college days. The size of his dick had been the stuff of urban legends even before he started his first term at Yale. A snort left his lips when a high-pitched voice started singing *"Monsta Beat! Monsta Beat!"* in the background behind his sister.

"Oh God," Julia groaned. "No, Lucas. We don't say Monster Meat—*shit*—I mean Monsta Beat—"

Lincoln bit the inside of his cheek as Julia's two-year-old son and Lincoln's favorite person in the whole world shouted, *"Shit Monsta Meat! Shit Monsta Meat!"* while Julia groveled at him to shut up.

"I'm gonna go, Linc," Julia said in a harassed voice. "Adam's gonna kill me if his darling son and the apple of his eye is still saying Monster Meat tonight. His boss is coming over for dinner."

Lincoln grinned. "Have fun explaining to your husband why your son keeps talking about his uncle's dick."

"Trust me, no one was more overwhelmed by your, er, package than Adam the one time he accidentally saw it in the tennis court changing rooms at Yale," Julia said with a grunt. "I swear he wanted to pen a poem about the damn thing for days after."

Lincoln chuckled and ended the call, cutting off the sound of his nephew hollering *"Shit Monsta Meat!"* at the top of his voice while his sister desperately tried to hush him. He'd just placed his cell phone on his desk when his secretary buzzed him.

"Yeah?" Lincoln said, his attention shifting to the widescreen computer in front of him.

"You need to come out here, NOW!" Barnaby Wodehouse hissed in a conspiratorial voice worthy of an Academy Award.

Lincoln frowned as he scrolled down the document he'd been reading before his sister called. "Why?"

He'd grown accustomed to Barnaby's dramatics since the young man started working for him three years ago. Although Lincoln had had his reservations when he'd first interviewed the flamboyant Cambridge graduate with the orange leather shoes and pink streaked blond hair, he'd been pleasantly surprised to discover that Barnaby more than lived up to his impressive resume. The fact that the guy could literally charm the skin off a snake had even helped many of Lincoln's business endeavors.

"The owner of *Le Secret* is here to see you," Barnaby

whispered, his British accent surfacing as it always did when he was excited about something.

It took a second for Lincoln to place the name *Le Secret*. His frown deepened. The whole reason he was in Tokyo right now was because he was focusing on expanding the Hudson Group into Asia and the Pacific. When the chance came up for him to buy a piece of prime land in the most exclusive district in Tokyo a few months ago, Lincoln knew it was the golden opportunity he'd been waiting for to build his flagship hotel in the city that never slept. The latest showpiece, as it were, in the chain of luxury hotels and resorts that took the world by storm a decade ago.

At the time he'd started the Hudson Group, Lincoln had three hundred grand to his name from bonds his mother had invested for him since he was a child. He quadrupled that figure in his first six months of business and continued to do so every year after that. That he was now worth over eight hundred times more than his father's net assets wasn't something Lincoln took particular delight in. He'd made sure Harry Hudson stayed off his radar after he walked out of the family home twelve years ago and had religiously disassociated himself from any business dealings where the other party wanted to exploit the benefit of a second-hand relationship with a serving U.S. senator.

It wasn't until Lincoln arrived in Tokyo ten days ago that he came to know the plot of land he'd bought in Ginza had a right to lease on it. He'd asked his legal team to investigate the matter and send the leaseholder's lawyers a formal notice to tell them their rights were being revoked. All Lincoln knew of *Le Secret* was that it was some kind of agency providing paid escorts to the highest bidder. The fact that its owner had managed to lease such a prime piece of real estate in Tokyo was nothing short of a miracle, which made Lincoln all the more doubtful about the exact nature of the services being provided by the woman who owned it. The phone call his secretary had received from *Le Secret*'s legal team yesterday had only reaffirmed Lincoln's suspicions. If *Le Secret*'s owner thought for one minute that he would buy the cock and bull story her lawyers had concocted about having been duped into buying what she'd assumed was the freehold to the land, then the woman had another thing coming.

Lincoln swiped a finger across his track pad and brought up his schedule for the day.

"Does she have an appointment?" he said coolly as he perused his digital calendar. "Because I can't see one."

"She doesn't," Barnaby replied. "She just turned up."

Lincoln narrowed his eyes. "Well, tell her she can make one then."

"Lincoln, just get the fuck out here!" Barnaby growled.

The buzzer went dead. Lincoln sighed.

He knew Barnaby would make his life difficult for the rest of the day if he didn't deal with the secretary's supposed emergency. He closed down his computer screen, rose reluctantly from his desk, and crossed his office. Lincoln opened the door and stepped out into his private lobby. Which, right now, didn't appear to be so private judging by the number of employees lurking at the periphery of the bright space and looking in from the adjoining corridors.

Lincoln's gaze landed on the elderly figure sitting on the couch directly opposite him and next to Barnaby's desk. He blinked. The woman was dressed in a pale tweed outfit and low pumps. Her hair was up in some kind of fifties do and she clutched a granny purse in her veiny hands. Thick-rimmed glasses covered her rheumy, distracted eyes and her rose-colored lipstick was slightly smudged.

Lincoln studied her with rising awe.

Wow. She must have been a firecracker in her heyday to be running an escort service. Lincoln's heart sank in the next instant. He masked a grimace. *Shit, this is gonna be unpleasant.*

Dexter, one of the Hudson Group's accountants, appeared in Lincoln's line of sight. He walked past Barnaby's desk and leaned down to offer a glass of water to the woman on the couch.

"Here you are, Aunt May. Hmm, wanna come to my office?" Dexter mumbled.

"In a minute," the old lady whispered loudly. She slipped a butterscotch out of her handbag and popped it into her mouth, her gaze focused unblinkingly on something to her right as she started sucking on the candy.

Lincoln gave Barnaby a puzzled frown.

The secretary jerked his head subtly toward the opposite side of the airy floor, his hazel eyes sparkling with shocked delight and a hint of devilry.

It was then that Lincoln realized that everyone, including Dexter and Dexter's aunt by the exchange he'd just heard, was staring goggle-eyed at the same spot just around a blind corner of the lobby, where the late morning sun shone through the glass facade of the high-rise building housing the local branch of the Hudson Group and offering a dizzying view over midtown Tokyo. Lincoln took a step forward, curious as to who or what had captivated everyone's attention.

He heard her before he saw her. His gaze swung south and found the cause of the impatient tapping noise he'd just registered.

The first thing Lincoln noticed were the shoes. They were traffic-light red, leather Manolo Blahnik stilettos made to hug a woman's feet and designed to inspire a man's dick to pay attention. The ball of the left one was dancing a restless tune against the marble floor of the lobby.

The next thing Lincoln registered were the black, see-through stockings with a solid seam running up the back of the most beautiful legs he had ever seen, legs that disappeared enticingly under an above-knee, navy blue, pinstripe pencil skirt that wrapped around a stunning ass and shapely hips.

Lincoln allowed his gaze to roam up the delicious dip of the woman's lower back and her rolled-up sleeved, black silk blouse, vaguely aware that he was growing hard. Sunlight cast a golden halo around her head and the cascade of luxurious, pale blond hair tumbling past her slim shoulders to the bottom of her delicate shoulder blades.

The tapping noise suddenly stopped. The woman straightened stiffly. She uncrossed her arms, her left hand clenched tightly on the handle of her cherry-colored Prada bag where she lowered it by her side.

Lincoln knew instinctively that she was staring at him through the reflection in the glass. How he was certain she was looking at him in particular and not the other men ogling her from across the lobby Lincoln wasn't sure since she was wearing sunglasses, but he was willing to wager a significant sum of money that her eyes were focused on him.

She twisted slowly on her heels and faced him across the open floor. Diamonds glinted in the clip-on earrings on her earlobes. Her breasts were lusciously full, her nose pert and slightly upturned, her lips plump and crowned by a perfect Cupid's bow, and her lipstick ruby red.

All the blood in Lincoln's body went south. He held his breath as the jaw-droppingly gorgeous stranger crossed the lobby and stopped in front of him.

The woman pushed her sunglasses up onto her head, her stilettos bringing her slender, five-foot-six body just high enough to his own hulking six-foot-two frame for her to only have to tilt her chin up to fix him with an electric blue stare.

Lincoln's dick pressed up uncomfortably against his zipper when he caught a hint of the perfume wafting enticingly off her golden skin in subtle waves. He detected Jasmine and Lily of the valley, as well as a musk base note.

"Lincoln Hudson?" the woman said coldly.

Her voice was deep and commanding, with a hint of huskiness that made his mouth water. Since speech seemed a bit beyond him at the moment, Lincoln could only arch an eyebrow in response and pray to God he wasn't drooling.

The woman frowned slightly. "Eveline Claude." She marched past him and headed inside his office. "Let's talk."

Lincoln took a shallow breath. *Fuck.*

He met his secretary's gleeful stare and knew Barnaby had guessed what was going on inside his mind.

There was only one word to describe Lincoln's reaction to Eveline Claude, the owner of *Le Secret* and, by the looks of it, the woman dying to tear him another asshole judging by the anger he'd read in the icy depths of her eyes.

Instalust.

CHAPTER THREE

*S*HIT.

Eveline fought to control the shiver of awareness running down her spine when she heard the door close behind her. She crossed her arms and turned to stare at the man facing her across the room, her heart pounding against her ribs.

Why does this asshole have to be completely and utterly, one hundred and fifty percent my type?

The last thing Eveline had expected when she'd turned up unannounced at the Tokyo branch of the Hudson Group to face her nemesis in the case of her misappropriated piece of real estate was that the man who owned the damn place was going to be a mouthwatering hunk. And not just any kind of hunk. Lincoln Hudson was the epitome of Eveline's perfect man. Thick, wavy brown hair crowned his six-foot-two, solid frame. He was classically handsome, the hard lines and rugged masculine angles of his face making him look like some mythological God or hero on a bust chiseled by a sculptor from Ancient Greece. Then, there were his eyes. They were hands down the clearest shade of ice-blue Eveline had ever seen on a human being. Add to this his stupidly broad shoulders, a ripped chest that spoke of a regular workout routine, and long legs she would happily worship all day, and Eveline knew she was in trouble.

The fact that Lincoln Hudson also appeared to be in possession of the most impressive package Eveline had ever spotted on a man wasn't helping matters.

It had been months since she'd last had sex, and the damp heat between her thighs told her she had a serious case of the hots for the guy gazing at her silently from the doorway of his office.

He moved then, his steps long and casual as he headed for the business end of the sleek desk dominating the space in front of the panoramic glass walls overlooking the city.

"Take a seat," Lincoln murmured, folding his sinfully gorgeous body into the executive chair behind the table.

Eveline reluctantly lowered herself into one of the two chairs facing his. She removed a file from her bag and slid it across the desk toward him.

Lincoln ignored the folder and eyed her with a haughty expression. "What's this?"

Eveline clenched her jaw. "The deeds to the land I bought off Nagato five years ago."

Lincoln narrowed his eyes slightly before pulling the file across and opening it.

Eveline found her gaze drawn to his long, elegant

fingers as he slowly riffled through the document she'd brought from Brooks & Kline.

I wonder how those would feel on my skin.

She tugged her lower lip unconsciously between her teeth when a torrid vision suddenly flashed through her mind. Of this man's hands on her body. Of his strong frame crushing her own delicate one in bed while he thrust his impossibly thick, rock-hard cock repeatedly inside her and made her cry out in ecstasy. Of his lips and tongue wreaking havoc on the most intimate part of her, bringing her to one blinding orgasm after another. Of him taking her and making her his in every wicked, sinful way a man could possess a woman.

Heat flooded Eveline's entire body and arrowed in on the aching space between her thighs. She crossed her legs and hoped to hell the man across the desk hadn't noticed how aroused she was right now.

LINCOLN STIFLED A GROAN OF DESIRE WHEN HE SAW Eveline chew her lower lip. She didn't seem to be aware she was doing it, which made the move all the more sexy. Lincoln realized there was a good chance he was going to embarrass himself and come inside his expensive cotton briefs if he didn't do something to calm his raging libido in the next minute.

He had never been so turned on in his life. In fact, there was only one thing Lincoln could think about right now. And that was to get up, walk around his desk, bend Eveline Claude over the table, lift her skirt up, and sink his throbbing dick so hard and deep inside her she'd scream with the pleasure of his possession. Then he'd do it over and over again until her voice was raw and they were both drenched in sweat and thoroughly sated.

It took all Lincoln's willpower to force himself to concentrate on the paperwork at hand. His stomach dropped when the contents of the contract started to sink in. If what he was reading was correct, then Eveline Claude had indeed been conned into purchasing a very expensive piece of land that she did not rightly own.

Lincoln went over the deeds twice before finally looking at the woman before him.

"I can see where this could be a problem," he said quietly. "However, that doesn't change the fact that that plot is now legally mine."

Eveline's expression grew shuttered.

"*Le Secret* has been established there for five years," she said in a steady voice. "It's my most successful club after New York and London. And I would like for it to remain so."

Lincoln's interest piqued as he studied the woman seated across from him. He was fast realizing that there was more to Eveline Claude than just a pretty face and a hot body. The light smoldering in the depths of her blue eyes told him she was probably as savvy a businesswoman as he was a businessman and that she didn't suffer fools lightly. He concealed his deepening curiosity and cocked an eyebrow at her.

"What are you suggesting?"

THE SEXY WAY LINCOLN ARCHED HIS EYEBROW AT HER made Eveline want to climb over the desk, haul him close by the front of his expensive Ralph Lauren shirt, and kiss him hard.

Sweet Mother of God, I'm losing my fucking mind!

Eveline took a shallow breath and pinched the back of her right wrist subtly where she'd crossed her hands on her knee. The sharp sting brought things back into focus. She realized Lincoln was waiting for her answer.

"I am in a position to buy you off," Eveline said. "As in, I want the freehold for that plot."

Lincoln blinked. He leaned back in his chair and swiveled it slightly as he considered her.

"Really?" he drawled. "And how much are you willing to offer me for it?"

Eveline hesitated before naming a figure, aware Brooks and Kline would have skinned her alive for being so reckless had they been in the room. She was shrewd enough a businesswoman to know that it was too early to reveal her full cards to the enemy. But, right now, she was desperate.

She couldn't afford to lose the Tokyo branch of *Le Secret*. Besides the fact that it would take a huge chunk out of her profits and jeopardize the livelihood of many of her local staff, she'd worked too damn hard to make it a success. It was also her favorite club of all her businesses.

Lincoln stared at her incredulously. A bark of laughter finally escaped his lips.

"Hell no! That land is worth twice that. Besides, I would never sell it."

＆

EVELINE NARROWED HER EYES AT HIM IN THE TENSE silence that followed. "Then, lease it to me."

Lincoln frowned at her demanding tone. He had an inkling Eveline was used to getting her own way. Which was a pity. Lincoln didn't like being told what to do, either inside or outside the bedroom. In fact, he very much enjoyed being the one who gave the orders, especially in bed. His cock throbbed as the urge to make this woman submit to him suddenly filled him.

"I have plans for that plot and leasing it to another business isn't part of it," he said, his voice turning cool.

Eveline stiffened. "So, you're saying you're not willing to negotiate?"

Since Lincoln couldn't very well say, *"I'd be willing to negotiate an arrangement where I get to fuck you at any time of day or night starting right this minute,"* he contented himself with shrugging.

Eveline rose to her feet and placed her hands palms down on the edge of Lincoln's desk.

"I'll increase that offer by thirty percent," she said icily. "That's my final bid."

Lincoln's dick ached at the way Eveline's breasts jutted forward slightly. He could just about make out her lacy black camisole beneath her blouse.

"The answer is still no," he said.

Eveline inhaled shakily and closed her eyes. The fury in their depths when she opened them once more made Lincoln's pulse spike.

God, she's fucking beautiful when she's mad.

Her next words drenched his libido as effectively as a bucket of ice.

"*You asshole!*" Eveline hissed. "I won't offer you a cent more than that. The offer expires at midday tomorrow. After that, I will drag your ass and the Nagatos into court if I have to." A grim smile curved her lips. "I bet your senator father would just love that!"

EVELINE KNEW INSTANTLY IT HAD BEEN THE WRONG thing to say. The way Lincoln turned to stone at the mention of his father and the rage that darkened his eyes to a stormy blue told her she'd just gone a step too far.

She'd done some research on Lincoln before she'd stormed over to his office that morning. She had unearthed his political connection to U.S. senator Harry Hudson pretty rapidly and had read up on his dizzy rise to fame and fortune from his mid-twenties with a degree of fascination. Despite the fact that they were in completely different lines of work, Lincoln's path over the last decade had followed hers closely, his business acumen and drive mimicking hers. And it was clear to her that Lincoln hadn't used his father's reputation to get where he was today.

Along with information of the Hudson Group's rapid expansion and the many awards the business had won since its creation, Eveline had come across tidbits of gossip involving the man himself. Lincoln had dated some pretty public figures in the past, including several models and actresses. What was interesting was the fact that he had always been the one who had broken off the brief liaisons. He was evidently not into long-term relationships.

"Don't bring my father into this," Lincoln growled.

A shiver danced across Eveline's skin at the fire in Lincoln's eyes and the electric tension filling the space between them. Even though she knew she'd pissed him off, she couldn't help the flash of desire that twisted her belly at his dominating tone.

Lincoln in complete command was a massive turn on.

Eveline swallowed and collected her bag from the floor.

"Midday tomorrow," she repeated in a steely voice that masked her disquiet. She slid her sunglasses back down onto her nose and gazed at the man behind the desk. "Your secretary knows how to reach me. My lawyers will be in touch after that deadline."

She turned and headed for the door, amazed her legs weren't shaking at the hot energy radiating off the furious man behind her.

LINCOLN LET OUT A RAGGED BREATH AND RAKED A HAND through his hair when the door thudded closed after Eveline.

His skin felt raw and his muscles quivered with the fury that still filled him. But, more than fury, Lincoln was shocked by the lust that still burned through him. Even though he was mad at Eveline for bringing up his father, his rock-hard erection was proof that he was still very much attracted to her.

The door opened. Barnaby walked in. He stopped and blinked when he saw Lincoln's face.

"Whoa," the secretary muttered. "Someone's rattled your cage."

Lincoln ignored the ache in his groin and frowned. "Get your hands on everything you can find out about Eveline Claude and *Le Secret*."

Barnaby smiled shrewdly. "This for business or pleasure?"

Lincoln hesitated. "Business."

Barnaby raised his eyebrows. "You sure? 'Cause, let me tell you, as a bisexual, I wouldn't mind a piece of *that* action."

Lincoln rolled his eyes. "The woman would eat you for breakfast, so don't even go there. Besides, I get the feeling she'd sell your skinny ass to the highest bidder if it made her a profit."

Barnaby grinned. "She can have my ass all day long."

Lincoln's frown deepened.

"Alright, alright, I'm going," Barnaby muttered.

The secretary returned two hours later with a

dossier on the woman who had stormed into Lincoln's office that morning and left him with a major hard-on.

Lincoln spent half his afternoon reading up on Eveline Claude, aka Madame Claude, and all her business endeavors. By the time he finished with the last file, he was wearing a grim smile.

He'd been right about Eveline. She was brilliant at business, just like he was. And she loved to play hardball, just like he did.

Lincoln swiveled his chair around and stared at the golden light bathing Tokyo, the idea that had been simmering at the back of his mind finally taking shape. He knew just what to do to address the problem that was Eveline Claude. And he was looking forward to the look on her face when he made his counter offer to her tomorrow. That it would infuriate her just as badly as she'd angered him when she'd mentioned his father was a given.

Lincoln grinned. His trip to Tokyo had just become doubly enjoyable. He was determined to have as much fun as possible with the feisty blonde who'd come onto his radar. And by the time he was done with her, she was going to regret ever crossing his path.

CHAPTER FOUR

"Honestly, the guy's a giant dick," Eveline said in a clipped voice into her cell phone.

Ethan Skye chuckled at the other end of the line.

He'd called her just as she'd walked through the door of her apartment at seven that evening. Worn out by the day's events and in need of a long, cold drink and company, Eveline had almost gone over to *Saron* when she'd left *Le Secret*. An exclusive gay club owned by Ethan's boyfriend Joe Cavendish, who also happened to be a close friend of Eveline's and a former male escort for her business, *Saron* was the place where Ethan worked as a bartender.

Not that he needed the job.

Known as Mr. S in the stock market, Ethan was a genius who'd amassed a fortune worth five times that of Eveline's in as many years. Although Joe had repeatedly told Ethan he didn't have to carry on working at *Saron* after they got together, Ethan still chose to do so. Mostly because he liked to be able to get in Joe's pants any time of night and day, but also because he really enjoyed his job, something the club's patrons were more than grateful for. Ethan was a world class bartender and people lined up at the doors to drink his cocktails. It didn't hurt that he was very easy on the eyes, a fact that caused Joe plenty of jealous moments whenever someone tried to get close to his precious boyfriend.

Eveline was still surprised at how quickly she and Ethan had become attached to one another. When she'd heard that Joe had put his own life at risk to protect a new employee from a stalker over a year ago, she'd gone over to *Saron* to check out the mysterious bartender who had apparently gotten through the walls Joe had built around his heart. She'd liked the feisty, green-eyed blond from the moment he'd opened his mouth and told her in no uncertain terms what she could do with her opinion, after she'd played devil's advocate to test his feelings for Joe. That Ethan was just as in love with Joe as Joe was with him had been evident from the get go, and Eveline relished that she was the one who had given the two men the final little nudge to consummate their relationship.

Ethan was very much the little brother she'd never had, and their relationship had only grown in strength over the last year. He was her shopping and lunching buddy, as well as her unofficial financial advisor when it came to her stocks and shares investments.

"Is he a giant dick or, you know, a *giant dick*?" Ethan said.

Eveline rolled her eyes at the overt innuendo as she

left the marble foyer and entered her open plan condo. "Are you seriously asking me whether I've checked out my enemy's junk?"

"Well, yeah. You'd investigate the Hunchback of Notre Dame's dick, you're so horny these days," Ethan said blithely.

"Hmm." Eveline headed into the kitchen and grabbed a bottle of Chardonnay from the wine cooler. "I bet Esmeralda would have fainted if she'd seen Quasimodo's package."

"So?" Ethan said impatiently.

"So what?" Eveline muttered distractedly, her hand stilling on a corkscrew as an image of Lincoln flashed before her eyes. Her belly tightened instantly with desire, a fact that irritated the hell out of her.

"You haven't answered the dick question," Ethan said.

Eveline sighed, tucked the phone between her shoulder and her ear, and popped the cork off the wine bottle. "Yes, he is disproportionately…big."

Ethan sucked air between his teeth. "Like, bigger than Joe?"

Eveline groaned. "I can't believe you just asked me that." She grabbed a wine glass from a cabinet and poured the sparkling liquid into it.

"I like big dicks and I cannot lie," Ethan said, paraphrasing one of their favorite karaoke songs. "Not that I'd swap Joe for anyone," he added hastily. "I mean, I could spend all day waxing lyrical about that man's—"

The sound of a scuffle broke out across the connection. Ethan cursed.

Eveline took a sip of her wine and grinned when another man came on the line.

"I'm sorry, I'm afraid Ethan's gonna have to call you back," Joe Cavendish said silkily.

She heard Ethan groan in the background.

"You've got him over your shoulder like a caveman again, haven't you?" Eveline said with a chuckle. She headed into the lounge and dropped into a black, leather Barcelona chair.

"You know me well," Joe said, amused.

There was a faint thwacking noise in the background. It was followed by an outraged cry.

"*Did you just spank me?!*" Ethan squealed.

"That's what you get for even thinking about another man's dick," Joe said. "And I'll be doing more than just spank you before the night is over."

"Oh God," Ethan moaned.

Eveline giggled. She knew Ethan loved it when Joe went all alpha on him.

"I'm gonna have to go, Evie," Joe said distractedly. "This kid needs a lesson about who he belongs to."

"But—but I'm still on my break!" Ethan protested in the background.

"Akihito and the others can cover for you," Joe said with grunt.

Eveline was still grinning when the call disconnected. She was reaching down to slide her right shoe off her foot when her cell rang again. She frowned when she saw the number. She straightened and took another sip of her wine before tapping the answer button.

"Hello?"

"Hi, Miss Claude?" someone said at the other end of the line in accented English.

"Speaking," Eveline said briskly.

"This is Yashiro Nakamura, head of parking security for the building."

"Oh. Hi, Yashiro," Eveline said, her tone warming. She'd gotten to know the apartment complex's management team over the three years she'd been living there. "How's that grandson of yours doing?"

"He's doing great, thanks for asking, Miss Claude," Nakamura said, his voice ringing with pride.

Eveline smiled faintly. Nakamura's grandson was a rising star in the Japanese university baseball league. From what Nakamura had told her over the last six months, he had a real chance at winning a contract with one of the major teams at tryouts this year.

"About the incident you reported to my staff this morning," Nakamura continued. "We've identified the owner of the vehicle who scratched your car and informed him of the incident. He was genuinely surprised and has offered to make amends. It seems he accidentally knocked his golf bag against your Maserati when he swung it out of the boot of his vehicle last night and didn't notice the damage in the dark."

Eveline raised an eyebrow. *Well, that's the first plus of the day.*

"Have you got his number?" she asked. "I'll call him tomorrow and—"

"If it's convenient for you, Mr. Hudson has informed me that he's more than happy to meet with you this evening and come to a personal arrangement, Miss Claude."

Eveline froze. *No way. It can't be—*

"Mr. Hudson?" she repeated carefully.

"Yes," Nakamura replied. "Mr. Hudson is the new penthouse tenant. He moved in last week."

Eveline's mouth went dry. *Please God, let it not be him.*

"What's his first name?" she said hoarsely.

"Excuse me?" Nakamura said, surprised.

"Mr. Hudson's first name. What is it?" Eveline mumbled.

"His full name is Mr. Lincoln Hudson."

Eveline swore.

CHAPTER FIVE

THE DOORBELL RANG AT EXACTLY SEVEN EIGHTEEN.

Lincoln's lips curved in an amused smile as he glanced at his watch.

That was fast.

The bell buzzed again. He took a sip of his scotch and headed leisurely across his apartment. His grin widened when the bell rang a third and fourth time. The caller evidently had reached the limit of their patience as they started pounding heavily on the door next.

Lincoln knew exactly who was on his doorstep and he was intent on savoring every second of what was to follow.

He reached the foyer, unlocked the entrance to his penthouse, and swung the thick mahogany panel open. He leaned casually against the wood and crossed his ankles as he studied the red-faced woman opposite him.

"*You fucking asshole!*" Eveline roared.

She stormed past him, her cell phone and apartment key in hand.

Lincoln swallowed a chuckle. His cock stirred as Eveline's perfume wafted across his nostrils.

"Come on in," he drawled over his shoulder.

He closed the door and headed after Eveline as she stomped inside his lounge. She stopped abruptly in the middle of the marble floor and spun around to face him, locks of wavy blonde hair whirling to frame her high cheekbones.

"That's a brand-new car!" she spat.

Remorse flashed through Lincoln at her accusing tone. He'd genuinely been unaware of the damage he'd inadvertently caused to the blue Maserati he'd parked next to last night when he'd come home. He'd only been renting the penthouse for ten days and he was still getting used to the place.

He'd been riding the elevator to his apartment that evening when the head of the building's parking security called him and told him about the incident. Lincoln had immediately agreed to pay for the cost of the repair.

To say that he was stunned when he'd learned the identity of the Maserati's owner would be a gross understatement. Lincoln was quick to realize that Fate had thrown him a bone. Shrewd predator that he was, he'd snatched it right up and fully intended to relish every tasty morsel, down to the very marrow.

"Yeah, I'm sorry about that," Lincoln said. "I'll get Barnaby to arrange to have it fixed tomorrow."

Eveline blinked, surprise widening her eyes. "Oh," she mumbled. "Hmm, okay."

Lincoln bit the inside of his cheek to stop himself from laughing at her suddenly deflated expression. He was surprised to discover that he was very much looking forward to getting to know this woman, and not just because she was smoking hot.

His anger at what she'd said to him that morning had faded by the time he'd left the office. Lincoln had grudgingly had to admit that Eveline couldn't have known how much he hated the very mention of his father's name and had likely had no idea the reaction it would engender when she'd taunted him with her threat. That she would fight dirty didn't surprise him. He would have done the same thing had he been in her shoes.

What hadn't changed, however, was his determination to bed her. Which was why he was still going to make her a counter offer he knew wouldn't please her.

❦

EVELINE DRAGGED HER GAZE FROM THE ENTICING glimpse of Lincoln's bare chest. He'd undone his tie and left the ends hanging casually loose. The blue silk matched his eyes and framed the V of his neck where he'd unfastened the top two buttons of his shirt. His skin was tanned and lightly freckled, the smattering of visible hair making her want to rip the material off his body and rake her fingers through the crisp, dark curls.

She forced an aloof expression on her face to hide the sudden flash of desire coursing through her, placed her hands on her hips, and turned slowly.

"You haven't done much with the place," she said critically as she inspected the penthouse.

The apartment was a separate, open-plan, concrete and glass construction set over two stories atop the condominium. It was enclosed by a wooden deck that framed an L-shaped swimming pool and a rooftop garden offering a dazzling, 360-degree-view of Tokyo.

The inside was an interior designer's dream. Marble floors contrasted elegantly with white-washed walls alternating with dark wood paneling, giving the place a unique, contemporary feel. Scattered throughout the airy living areas were sleek, made-to-order furnishings and contemporary art pieces that looked like they had a five-figure price tag. The whole place was bathed in clever lightning and kitted out with top of the line electrical goods that screamed money.

What it lacked were personal touches. She couldn't see any sign of the infuriating man who'd charged into her life that morning and who was fast becoming the subject of every filthy fantasy she'd ever had.

"You've visited the penthouse before?" Lincoln asked curiously.

Eveline rolled her eyes at him. "*Everyone's* visited the penthouse. It's the building showpiece." She chewed her lip. "I would have bought the place myself three years ago if it wasn't so ludicrously expensive. I didn't know they were renting it—"

She gasped when her gaze landed on the state-of-the-art kitchen to her right. More precisely, it narrowed in on the blackened remains of a metal contraption.

§

Lincoln followed Eveline's line of sight, puzzled. He grimaced when he registered what had captured her attention.

"*You!*" she hissed. She dragged her eyes from the evidence of his one shortcoming in life and pointed a finger at him. "*You're the asshole with the waffle maker!*"

Lincoln rubbed the back of his neck. "Yeah, well, gadgets aren't really my thing," he muttered awkwardly.

He'd never mixed well with technology, something his sister and his few close friends delighted in teasing him about. His housekeeper back in New York had even banned him from using any of the labor-saving devices in his home after he set the juicer on fire.

The incident with the waffle maker that morning had hardly come as a surprise.

Eveline opened and closed her mouth soundlessly. She uttered an outraged sound, marched over to the well-appointed, circular bar set against the west wall of the lounge, and grabbed a bottle of Scotch from the shelf. She poured herself a generous amount, eyeballed the level of the spirit with a scowl, and doubled it. She dropped a couple of ice cubes in the tumbler before climbing onto a stool and gulping half the drink.

Lincoln watched, amused, as she slumped face down over the counter and groaned.

"You okay?" he asked, glancing at the expanse of stocking-covered, golden flesh exposed by Eveline's skirt where it's ridden up her thighs.

Fuck. What I wouldn't give to have those legs wrapped around my waist right now.

Eveline shoved her left middle finger at him where she lay across the counter. "No. I've had a shitty day and it's all thanks to you, Mr. Dickhead Hudson."

Lincoln chuckled at the insult. He glanced toward the kitchen.

"Have you eaten yet?" he said impulsively.

Eveline raised her head slowly and looked at him, her expression incredulous. A suspicious frown marred her brow in the next instant.

"No. Why are you asking?" she said warily.

"If you don't mind waiting, I can rustle up something quick," Lincoln said, masking his own surprise behind a light tone.

That he'd even suggested making dinner for Eveline took him aback. He was a private person and was always been particular about who he invited in his personal space.

Lincoln realized then that he didn't want Eveline to leave.

Eveline arched an eyebrow at him in response. Taking that as a yes, Lincoln strolled into the kitchen and headed over to the large, silver larder fridge.

Footsteps rose behind him as Eveline slowly followed. She settled in one of the counter chairs at the island dominating the floorspace while he eyed the well-stocked shelves of the fridge. Barnaby had hired a catering company for Lincoln's stay in Tokyo and there was enough food in the penthouse to feed an army.

"You like steak?" Lincoln paused and looked over his shoulder with a grimace. "Or are you one of those women who's stupidly strict about what they eat?"

"This body is no temple," Eveline said haughtily. "I like all kinds of meat."

Lincoln raised his eyebrows at the innuendo. Eveline took a sip of her Scotch before giving him a sexy, filthy smile. He chuckled and removed a marinated platter of steak and ingredients for a salad before setting them on the counter.

"Is that Kobe beef?" Eveline asked in an awed voice.

Lincoln grinned at her as he undid the plastic wrap. "It is. How do you like your steak?"

"Medium rare," Eveline murmured, her gaze glued to the thick slabs of meat on the plate.

Lincoln placed a large griddle pan on the ultra-modern cooking range and set it to preheat. He rolled up his sleeves, tugged his tie off, and hooked an apron over his neck.

A shutter click sounded from the direction of the island.

Lincoln looked around into Eveline's devilish grin. She had her cell phone camera aimed at him.

"What, you've never seen a man in an apron before?" he said testily.

Eveline chuckled. "Oh, I have. This is just blackmail fodder."

Lincoln shook his head, amused despite himself at her flagrant brazenness. He seasoned the steaks and placed them in the griddle pan before quickly preparing the salad, conscious of Eveline's curious stare.

"Why don't you pick a wine?" he murmured, indicating the glass facade of the wine cellar built inside the south wall of the kitchen.

Eveline downed her Scotch, slipped off the chair, and strolled over to the walk-in storeroom. She inspected the gallery of bottles for a moment before leaning down at the waist to select one from the lowest shelf.

Lincoln swallowed a groan at the tantalizing vision of Eveline bent over in her red stilettos, her pert ass stretching her tight, pinstriped skirt in all the right places, and the back of her long, mouthwatering thighs exposed. He caught a glimpse of her lacy, black garter belt and felt his cock throb.

At this rate, he was going to have a permanent hard-on during dinner.

Oblivious to the growing ache in Lincoln's groin, Eveline returned with a Red Bordeaux and two wine glasses. He handed her a corkscrew he found in a drawer and saw her smile faintly when she glanced at the brand new, gleaming, electric wine opener standing forlornly on a granite worktop.

"Have you used it even once?" Eveline said, opening the bottle with an expert twist of the corkscrew.

The rich aroma of the wine reached Lincoln's nostrils above the tantalizing smell of the grilling meat.

"Nope," he grunted.

Lincoln slipped the steaks onto a wooden board when they were done, removed plates and cutlery from a sliding drawer, and took everything over to a dining table overlooking the rooftop garden and the colorful city beyond. Eveline followed leisurely in his steps and took the seat opposite him while he served the salad.

He sat down and accepted the glass of wine she offered him while they waited for the meat to cool. She leaned back in her chair and took a slow sip of the scarlet liquid.

"This is nice," she murmured, studying him with a steady expression.

Lincoln relaxed in the chair. He didn't think he'd mistaken the glint of interest in Eveline's eyes that morning. Even if he had, there was no mistaking what he could read in them right now.

The air thickened with sexual tension as Eveline held his stare. Her gaze dropped to his mouth. She licked her lips unconsciously.

Fire shot through Lincoln's dick at the sight of her pink, wet tongue. He bit back a growl of desire and forced a faint smile on his face.

"Shall I?"

CHAPTER SIX

Yes, God, please climb over this table and kiss me now!

Eveline bit her lip to stop the shameless words from leaving her mouth. Heat warmed her cheeks when she realized Lincoln was indicating the steaks, his amused expression telling her he knew exactly what she'd been thinking a second ago.

"Please do," she said in as regal a tone as she could muster.

Eveline was surprised at how easily the conversation flowed between them as they ate and drank over the next couple of hours. They talked about New York, where they'd both started their companies, and the ways in which they'd grown their respective businesses over the last decade. They discovered they had several acquaintances and interests in common and had even invested in the same portfolios on the stock market. Lincoln told Eveline about his sister Julia and his nephew, his affection for the little boy evident in his softening eyes and voice.

She noted he never spoke about his father or mother, even after he asked her about her own family.

"I never knew my dad," Eveline said casually. "He walked out on us when I was one. As for my mom, I haven't spoken to her in eighteen years." She looked up into Lincoln's questioning stare and smiled faintly. "She chose to side with my stepdad when I told her he tried to rape me."

Lincoln stiffened in his chair, his pupils dilating with shock and anger.

"Did you report him to the cops?" he said harshly.

"I couldn't," Eveline said with a shrug. "He'd already gone to the station by the time I thought about it."

A puzzled frown darkened Lincoln's face. "What do you mean?"

"I beat him up," Eveline said blithely. "Pretty badly."

Even now, the memory of what happened all those years ago burned brightly in Eveline's mind. She'd seen the creepy looks her stepfather had been giving her ever since she turned fifteen and blossomed almost overnight, her awkward, gangly teenage figure maturing into that of a woman.

She was eighteen the day he walked into her bedroom and pinned her to the mattress while her mother worked the late shift at the local 7-Eleven. That night, Eveline discovered a side of herself she didn't even know existed.

As her stepfather yanked her nightshirt up her thighs and shoved his hand inside her panties, his arm pressed against her throat and choking her, terror had frozen Eveline for a timeless moment. She'd stared up at the man she'd lived with for thirteen years through a haze of tears and seen a stranger. A stranger who was going to violate her and find a way to hide his despicable act. A stranger who didn't give a damn that he was going to leave her with an emotional scar that could take a lifetime to heal.

It was when he'd relaxed the arm across her throat briefly to grope her breasts that Eveline saw her opportunity to escape. She'd kneed him in the balls and jumped out of the bed while he cried out and curled up into a fetal position. She was running for the door when she saw her hockey stick standing against the wall next to the window. The expression on her stepfather's face when she stopped and snatched it up before turning around to face him was one Eveline would never forget.

It was only afterward that she'd realized she'd even used her fists during the red haze of fury that had been those life-changing minutes. That was when Eveline grasped something fundamental about herself and the person she would become.

She was a survivor, through and through.

After her mother called her a whore for seducing her stepfather, Eveline did the only thing she could do. She packed a bag, stayed the night at a friend's house, and left town the next morning with several hundred dollars she'd saved from her babysitting job.

"I took the Greyhound to New York and worked as

a waitress for a year before a friend introduced me to an escort service," Eveline said.

Lincoln watched her with an inscrutable expression.

"The incident with your stepdad didn't put you off sex?" he said after a short silence.

Eveline narrowed her eyes.

"Just so we're clear, I've never had sex for money," she said coolly. "And no, it didn't. I've always enjoyed the act and I saw no need for that bastard to ruin it for me."

Eveline didn't go into the details of how she'd relished pushing the boundaries of her sensuality when she started visiting New York's sex clubs and dungeons. Like she'd told Lincoln, she'd never slept with anyone purely for money, even when her clients offered her eye watering sums for the privilege of fucking her.

Eveline knew what she liked in the bedroom and she only slept with men who could satisfy her own sexual desires. She became a professional dominatrix by accident, after a client for the escort service she was working for at the time begged her to tie him up and spank him. The money she earned in the years that followed bought her a college education and allowed her to invest in her own escort club at the age of twenty-five.

Within a year, *Le Secret* became known as *the* place for wealthy businessmen and movie stars to hang out at in New York. The fact that most of her escorts were well-educated, glamorous men and women who knew the etiquette for every social situation wasn't an accident. The rigid, six-week long induction program Eveline had developed for her staff meant that by the time they hit the club floor, they knew how to dress, how to walk, how to make basic cocktails, what cutlery to use for an official dinner, and even what topics of conversation the club's clients preferred.

As to sex between her escorts and the men and women who paid for their services, Eveline had made it a rule that whatever happened behind closed doors was a strictly private matter between two consenting adults and nothing to do with her business. It was a requirement of all her clubs that both escorts and clients signed a contract stating just that before they were even allowed through the doors.

"And here you are, eleven years later, the head of your very own business empire," Lincoln said in an enigmatic voice.

Eveline gazed at him thoughtfully, unsure if he was being sardonic.

"So, you looked up my age," she murmured.

Lincoln's lips curved in a lopsided smile that brought out a pair of such heart-stoppingly cute dimples Eveline would have forgiven him anything then.

"Since you knew about my father, I can only presume you did the same," he drawled in an amused voice.

Eveline paused with her wine glass halfway to her lips. She lowered it to the table.

"You didn't like me mentioning his name earlier

today," she said carefully. "Is there bad blood between you?"

Lincoln's smile faded and his face darkened with emotion. For a moment, Eveline thought he would ask her to get up and leave.

"You're bold," he said stiffly.

Eveline smiled faintly. "And you're avoiding the question."

Lincoln frowned between lifting his glass and staring at the crimson liquid. "Let's just say the less I have to do with that man, the better." He looked up at Eveline and hesitated. "I hear you have a number of prominent politicians among your clientele."

"I do," Eveline said noncommittally. "And no, he isn't among them."

Something like relief flashed in Lincoln's eyes.

She grew pensive as she helped him clear the table and headed into the lounge with a second bottle of Bordeaux while he loaded the dishwasher.

There was more to Lincoln Hudson than met the eye. Despite the fact that he was her de facto enemy, Eveline couldn't deny her burning desire to discover the man behind the ruthless public persona he projected to the world.

Lincoln joined her on the black leather couch a moment later and took the glass she offered him.

"To new friendships," he murmured.

CHAPTER SEVEN

Eveline arched an eyebrow before raising her own glass in a toast.

"Are we friends?" she said, folding her legs under herself as she made herself comfortable.

"I'd like to think we could be," Lincoln said truthfully.

He was amazed at how relaxed he was in Eveline's company. Although he should have been wary of her considering the circumstances of their first meeting, he couldn't deny that the more he learned about her, the more he wanted to know. The fact that she had risen above the trauma of almost being raped by her stepfather and gone on to build such a successful career for herself in a fiercely competitive business that thrived on the most hedonistic aspects of human behavior was nothing short of astounding. Lincoln had known she was an astute business woman from the moment he'd met her and the report Barnaby had compiled for him earlier that day had only confirmed his gut feeling.

He now understood Eveline's drive to succeed and conquer every obstacle that had ever stood in her path. She was a fighter inside and out.

Which meant he was up against a bigger challenge than he'd anticipated.

Silence descended between them as they gazed at each other. It was superseded by a slow, burning tension. The same electrifying sexual heat Lincoln had felt since the moment he'd met Eveline.

Eveline's gaze grew hooded. "So, are we going to talk about the elephant in the room?"

A burst of laughter escaped Lincoln despite his growing erection.

"I like that about you," he chuckled before taking a sip of his wine.

Eveline arched her eyebrow at him, her lips curving into a lopsided smile. "What, my sassy mouth?"

Lincoln's gaze dropped to Eveline's full lips. "Yes. That and the fact that you're not afraid to speak your mind."

A hint of color bloomed on Eveline's cheekbones under Lincoln's stare.

"It's a habit that has landed me in hot water on many an occasion," she admitted ruefully.

"You don't say," Lincoln drawled. He knew he was responsible for the flush of awareness on Eveline's face. The fact that he was affecting her just as badly as she was him thrilled him to the core.

Eveline narrowed her eyes. "You're laughing at me, aren't you?"

Lincoln grinned. He was also fast discovering that teasing Eveline was fun.

"I'm laughing with you," he said in a conciliatory tone. "There's a difference." He reached over, took Eveline's wine from her, and placed their glasses on the coffee table.

Eveline gave him puzzled look. "Why did you do that?"

"Because I have a counter offer to make and I'm afraid you might throw your wine at me after you hear it," Lincoln said steadily.

An unusual bout of nervousness darted through him as he watched Eveline tense. It surprised Lincoln, just as so many things had tonight.

He was a man who was supremely confident in his own skin and how he managed his daily affairs. Yet, this woman had managed to faze him in more ways than anyone had ever done in the short time they'd known each other.

He wondered then whether he had finally met his match in Eveline Claude. That thought sobered him.

Lines marred Eveline's brow. "What do you mean a counter offer?"

"I'm in Tokyo for a month," Lincoln said calmly. "I want you to be my escort for the duration of my time here."

Eveline's eyes flared in shock. She blinked slowly.

"I'm sorry, what did you just say?!" she blurted, disbelief raising her voice to a high-pitched squeak.

Lincoln kept his expression neutral as he gazed at her. "I want you to be my escort while I'm in Tokyo," he repeated in a casual voice. "I'll pay for your services, obviously. I want to see exactly what *Le Secret* is about before I make a decision whether to lease the plot to you."

❧

EVELINE'S HEART THUDDED WILDLY AGAINST HER RIBS AS she gaped at Lincoln.

Did he just say that? He did, didn't he?

Her mind raced as she struggled to come up with a suitable comeback to Lincoln's bold proposition. Her first instinct had been to throw her wine in his face. That he had anticipated she would do just that and taken the glass from her made her even more angry with the damn man.

Yet, despite the fury burning through her, Eveline couldn't deny one fact. The words "Lincoln Hudson" and "escort" in combination were making her all kinds of hot.

She cursed her treacherous body and pinched her lips.

"You mean you want to buy me for a month? Like I said before, I'm not a whore," she snapped.

Lincoln draped one arm lazily along the back of the couch. "Trust me, I won't be paying you for sex, Eveline."

Something   that   felt   suspiciously   like disappointment flashed through Eveline then. *No. No, I don't feel let down by that. That would be insane!*

Lincoln's next sentence doused any misconception she had about his intentions.

"I'm pretty confident you'll be begging me to fuck you instead," he stated blithely.

Eveline drew a breath in sharply, shocked at the sheer arrogance of the man opposite her. She moved then, her body shifting of its own volition. She knelt on the couch, grabbed the ends of Lincoln's shirt collar, and yanked him toward her.

"Oh yeah? You sure you can satisfy me, Mr. Dickhead Asshole Hudson?" Eveline hissed.

She immediately regretted her action when Lincoln raised his hands and cradled her elbows in his palms.

Shit.

Heat blazed through Eveline's flesh at Lincoln's touch. He was far too close. She could feel his breath on her face. Could sense his body temperature through his clothes. Could see the fire darkening his ice-blue eyes to indigo.

"I know I'm going to make you scream louder than you've ever screamed before," Lincoln said, his voice dropping to a gravelly octave that raised goose bumps on Eveline's skin. His cheeks dimpled and his lips curved into the most devastatingly alluring smile Eveline had ever seen on a human being. He cocked an eyebrow. "And, by the way, my nickname in college was Monster Meat."

Eveline's pulse raced erratically as her gaze dropped

to Lincoln's very obvious erection. Wetness pooled instantly between her thighs.

"Fuck," she muttered before looking up wildly into Lincoln's heated stare.

They moved toward each other, their mouths meeting in a savage, scalding kiss that instantly robbed Eveline of the ability to think. An animal growl left Lincoln's throat as he sucked and tasted her for long, blistering seconds. He lowered his hands to her waist and pulled her onto his lap before parting her lips with a skillful thrust of his tongue.

Holy. Crap.

Eveline shivered and closed her eyes, her own tongue rising to lash sensually against Lincoln's as he explored her mouth, pleasure thrumming through her at the intimate dance of flesh. He cradled her head in his large hands and angled her face so he could delve inside farther, his fingers curling roughly in her hair while his breaths washed out of his nose in long, heavy pants.

Eveline moaned, her own hands shifting to Lincoln's wide shoulders, her fingers digging into his hard, toned flesh.

Lincoln wrenched his mouth from hers, nudged her chin up, and kissed a fiery trail down her throat to the sensitive skin covering the fluttering pulse at the base. His hands moved sensuously along her face and neck before dropping to cup her heavy breasts.

Eveline hummed and arched her head back as Lincoln flicked and rubbed her hard nipples with his thumbs through the thin material of her blouse. Her thighs tensed and her passage clenched as the faint pulses of an orgasm started building inside her. She bit her lip.

She couldn't believe she was nearing a climax just from Lincoln's touch and kiss.

He undid the top buttons of her blouse with an expert twist of his fingers and reached inside her camisole and lacy bra.

Eveline gasped when Lincoln palmed her naked flesh with his bare hands. Cool air washed across her feverish skin as he lifted her breasts free. A raspy moan ripped from her throat when he replaced his teasing thumbs with his mouth.

LINCOLN'S COCK THROBBED PAINFULLY BEHIND THE zipper of his pants.

He knew he'd be playing with fire when he touched Eveline. What he hadn't anticipated was that the blaze would swallow him whole so quickly. Eveline's lips. Her skin. Her body. The sounds she made as she rode her rising pleasure. All of it was driving him crazy with lust.

The smoky wine they'd been drinking was still evident on her tongue when he kissed her. And her skin. Christ, her skin was soft and oh so smooth, with the sweet flavor of vanilla. Whereas her breasts.

Fuck, her breasts taste like Heaven!

Lincoln groaned as he swirled his tongue and licked the stiff, pink nipples begging for his attention before sucking them deep inside his mouth one at a time, his thumb playing with the one his lips abandoned.

Shivers shook Eveline as she bowed her head and spine, her hips rolling instinctively against Lincoln's groin, her body seeking its release from the delicious tension he could feel building inside her. Lincoln worked Eveline's breasts with his left thumb and his mouth and reached down with his right hand.

Eveline stiffened when he slipped his fingers under her skirt. He trailed them along the inside of her right thigh, lingered on the quivering, silky skin he found above her lacy garter belt, and arrowed in on the burning apex of her thighs.

Lincoln cursed when he felt Eveline's damp panties against his fingertips and caught a whiff of her musky scent. He dipped his hand inside the silky material and cupped her sex.

Eveline's hair tickled the sides of Lincoln's face as she brought her head down and looked at him. Her face was flushed and her blue eyes so dark with passion he could barely see her pupils. The untamed expression on her face told him exactly what she wanted him to do right now.

Lincoln's pulse raced as he held Eveline's feral gaze. He pinched her right nipple, sucked on her left breast, and parted her wet, slick folds, exploring the most intimate part of her.

Eveline's breath froze when Lincoln's thumb found her clit at the same time he slid two fingers inside her tight, hot passage.

Her lips opened on a throaty moan as he rubbed her

sensitive nub with a slow, circular motion. She bit the inside of her cheek and clenched her inner muscles, squeezing his fingers where they invaded her body.

Lincoln's dick spasmed painfully.

Shit, I want inside her so bad!

He knew it was too soon for them to have full-on, penetrative sex. Not only did he think Eveline would come to regret it, Lincoln was determined to take his time and tease her long and slow to get what he wanted out of the bargain he wished to make with her about the plot of land in Ginza.

CHAPTER EIGHT

Eveline let out a frustrated sound when Lincoln's hand stilled on the throbbing space between her thighs.

The feel of his long, elegant fingers inside her and his thumb resting oh so tantalizingly on her clit were driving her insane. She rocked her hips against his hand, her gaze locked on his where he teased her breasts with his mouth and hand, silently urging him on.

"Say it, Eveline," Lincoln murmured against her skin.

Eveline blinked, her passion-addled brain stuttering in incomprehension for a moment.

Lincoln drew back slightly and flicked her left nipple roughly with his thick tongue. "Say you'll be my escort."

Electric tingles shot from Eveline's breast down to her aching passage. Her muscles spasmed around Lincoln's fingers, sucking him farther inside her body.

He hissed, his thumb and forefinger tightening on her right nipple in a punishing pinch that made her gasp with pleasure.

Lincoln frowned up at her. "Say it," he growled.

Eveline scowled. *This asshole!*

Her anger faded in the next instant as he tugged her left nipple between his teeth, withdrew his fingers from her passage, and thrust them back in slowly. Her nails bit into his shoulders and she cursed at the jolt of intense pleasure.

Lincoln stilled. "Eveline," he said in a warning tone.

Eveline stared dazedly at the man below her and knew he was more than willing to withhold her orgasm until she agreed to his crazy demand.

Her instincts told her she should climb off his lap and tell him exactly where he could shove his counter offer.

But something made her pause. Something that stunned her.

In all her years as an escort and dominatrix, Eveline had never submitted to a man. She had always been in charge of her own pleasure and had taken it whenever she wanted to. Being at Lincoln's mercy like this went against everything she had ever experienced or even thought she liked.

Yet, Eveline realized she had never been so turned on in her life as she was in that moment. And that revelation shocked her to the core.

That this stranger, a man she had met barely eleven hours ago, was controlling her body right now, was *making* her wait for an orgasm which she knew was going to blow her mind, was not only dictating the terms of this sexual encounter but a business arrangement that would affect both of them while his own splendid erection begged for attention, made her shiver with the need to surrender.

Lincoln watched her silently, his hands motionless on her body, his burning breath tormenting the sensitive flesh of her left breast. He must have read something on her face then as his eyes softened, the hardness in the ice-blue depths melting to such pure need and raw power Eveline couldn't help the shudder that raced down her spine.

"Say it," he whispered in a deep, seductive tone.

Eveline closed her eyes and let out a low whimper. "Yes."

A shocked cry left her lips when Lincoln dipped his head and swallowed her left nipple into his mouth. He sucked and swirled his tongue around the swollen nub, his hand busy working the other nipple.

Eveline grabbed the back of Lincoln's head and held on tight as he started working his magic down below, his thumb rubbing and rotating sensuously across her aroused clit while he started thrusting his fingers deep inside her.

Pleasure washed through Eveline, so intense it was almost pain. Her toes curled as the most incredible heat pooled deep inside her belly. She clenched around Lincoln's fingers and heard him snarl as he accelerated the motion of his hand, finger fucking and rubbing her toward her orgasm.

Eveline came with a fury that stunned her. Her

breath locked in her throat as the first violent pulse of her climax slammed into her. She trembled and opened her mouth on a harsh shout. Sound and sight faded when the next waves had her convulsing violently in Lincoln's firm hold, her body writhing and rolling helplessly against his while he continued driving his fingers inside her, prolonging her mind-numbing orgasm while her passion-filled cries echoed dimly in her ears.

It was some time before Eveline realized she was lying limply in Lincoln's arms, her head on his shoulder while her labored breaths shuddered in and out of her chest. She blinked.

He'd tucked her breasts back inside her blouse and was holding her gently against him, one hand cradling her lower back while the other supported her nape. Her throat constricted at the tender gesture so at odds with the masterful way he'd just played her body.

"How long was I out for?" Eveline said hoarsely. She raised her head, gripped his shoulders, and sat back slowly on her heels.

Lincoln dropped his hands to her waist. "About a minute."

Eveline flushed. There was no hiding the fact from the man before her that the orgasm he had just given her had been so intense she'd practically passed out from the pleasure of it.

Yet, she couldn't detect any scorn on Lincoln's face. Even though he had forced her to submit to him, the only thing Eveline could read in Lincoln's dark eyes was desire.

She shifted on his lap. A groan left his throat as her sex nudged against his bulging erection.

Eveline licked her lips, pushed up slightly on her knees where she straddled Lincoln's lap, and dropped a hand to his groin. His nostrils flared, his breaths washing out of him in short, harsh pants. Lincoln held Eveline's heated gaze as she slowly undid his belt buckle and pulled his zipper down.

In that moment, she knew he was allowing her control. She shivered at the power he'd given her, knowing he could take it back at any moment, yet certain he wouldn't.

A shudder ran through Lincoln when Eveline trailed a finger along his hard length. He cursed, yanked his briefs down, and grabbed her right hand. A hiss escaped his lips as he guided her fingers onto his naked cock.

Eveline swallowed convulsively as she finally beheld Lincoln's impossibly thick and magnificently engorged dick. He was so big he barely fit in her palm. His shaft was silky smooth and veiny, the flushed skin glistening with the pre-cum leaking at the broad, pink head while his trimmed pubes arrowed down to his balls where they rested heavily in their sac.

Her passage contracted at the thought of taking Lincoln deep inside her one day. That he would fill her to the very core and stretch her wider than she had ever been stretched before brought an instant flood of wetness to her sex.

Eveline's pulse thundered in her veins as she started stroking Lincoln. He moaned and closed his eyes briefly, color painting his cheekbones with red flags of pleasure. She found her breathing matching his as they stared unblinkingly at each other once more, excitement causing her to pant while she rubbed and kneaded his slick length.

More. I want more. I want to—

Eveline rose and climbed off Lincoln's lap. He sucked air between his teeth when she spread his thighs wide and dropped to her knees before him. Eveline leaned forward and did what she was dying to do in the moment.

A guttural sound left Lincoln when her lips closed around the sensitive head of his cock. The heady scent of Lincoln's arousal swamped Eveline's senses at the same time she tasted his intoxicating pre-cum. Her passage pulsed with a spasm of need. She licked and circled the tip of his shaft expertly with her tongue before cradling the base with her hands and taking him inside her mouth.

Lincoln tensed and rolled his hips reflexively as she started to suck him. His hands found the back of her skull, his fingers clenching in her hair as he fixed her head just where he wanted it.

Eveline looked up and smiled teasingly around Lincoln's stiff, trembling shaft while she swallowed him almost to the back of her throat.

Lincoln's pupils dilated above her, his expression growing wild with burning lust when he realized what she intended.

"Do it," he growled.

Eveline closed her eyes and gave Lincoln what they

both wanted so very badly, her head dipping sensuously up and down his quivering erection as she blew and deep throated him toward an orgasm.

Lincoln's fingers tightened painfully in her scalp when he came. Animal sounds rumbled out of his chest as he dropped his head back against the couch and thrust his cock powerfully into her eager mouth, ecstasy twisting his features in a savage mask. Eveline trembled when Lincoln's shaft throbbed and pulsed between her lips, flooding her mouth and throat with his thick cum. She swallowed and sucked the hot, sticky liquid to the last drop, her eyes locked on his sweat-slicked face and the powerful, corded muscles of his neck as he grunted and groaned in pleasure.

In that moment, Eveline knew she would never see anyone as beautiful as this man in the throes of passion, nor would she ever taste anything as addictive as the musky evidence of his climax.

CHAPTER NINE

"Wow." The pretty Asian girl who'd spoken blinked her large, black eyes at Eveline before grimacing. "You look like hell. Late night?"

"Kinda," Eveline said with a grunt to her assistant Yuki Harada where the latter sat behind her desk in the office above *Le Secret*. It was almost lunchtime and she'd just made it into the building.

Four days had passed since Eveline's torrid encounter with Lincoln at his penthouse. She'd left his place that night with the understanding that he would get in touch with her when he wanted to meet up and sign the contract to officially engage her services. He'd texted her the next morning to tell her something urgent had come up and he was leaving town to head back to the States. As the next two days passed with no further messages from Lincoln, Eveline wondered wildly whether he'd been playing her and had gone back on his word. It wasn't until Malcolm Brooks got in touch with her late on the afternoon of the third day to tell her *Le Secret*'s revocation order had been put on hold until further notice that Eveline finally heaved a sigh of relief.

"How did you do it?" Brooks said over the phone. "I could have sworn nothing would make that guy budge on his decision. He has a reputation for being a ruthless bastard."

Eveline had smiled grimly at the lawyer's words.

She still couldn't believe what had happened between her and Lincoln that night at his penthouse. As she analyzed the details of their blistering meeting in the cold light of day, the way she'd submitted so easily to him had troubled her to no end.

Regardless of the fact that she was insanely and stupidly attracted to Lincoln, Eveline was furious at herself for having given in so easily to the man.

There was no denying that he had some kind of magical hold on her; that he appeared to have weaved a spell that robbed her of her common sense and her usual cold-hearted determination when it came to engaging her enemy. Because, despite everything that Lincoln had said about becoming friends, there was no escaping the reality that they were both fighting over the same exclusive plot of land.

"It's amazing what a man's dick will make him do," Eveline had said tartly to the lawyer.

Brooks drew a sharp breath. "Oh, Jesus," he groaned. "You slept with him."

Eveline grimaced. "Technically, that's a no."

"But something happened?" Brooks said insistently.

"I'm gonna have to plead the Fifth on that one," Eveline said.

"Christ," Brooks muttered. "Just be careful, Eveline. I

know you're used to going up against the big boys, but this guy is, well—like the biggest of them all."

Eveline arched an eyebrow. "Don't I know it."

Brooks cursed under his breath. She'd berated herself for her crass words and managed to pacify the lawyer before ending the call.

She'd spent that night tossing and turning in bed as she wondered when Lincoln would contact her again. When dawn rose on the next day and there was still no message from the CEO of the Hudson Group, Eveline had called her assistant to tell her she was going to come in late and spent half the morning working out her growing frustration in the gym in her apartment building. She'd gone over to the private dojo where she practiced her kickboxing afterward and punched and kicked a sandbag until her body ached.

Even though Eveline had been fit from all the hockey and volley ball she'd played in high school, she'd taken up self-defenses classes shortly after she started living in New York and had discovered a natural affinity for that particular branch of martial arts. It had gotten her out of the occasional sticky situation during her years as an escort, when a client refused to understand that no meant no.

"Can you get me a coffee? Black, no sugar," Eveline said presently.

Yuki gave her a slow, wicked grin. "Sure, but only if you promise to tell me the name of the guy."

Eveline sighed before heading into her office. At nearly six feet, Yuki was tall for a Japanese girl. It was what had first attracted Eveline's eye when she started hiring female escorts for the Tokyo branch of *Le Secret* after setting up shop in the city five years ago. Although Yuki proved to be one of *Le Secret*'s top employees, Eveline quickly realized the girl's talents lay elsewhere. Not only was Yuki stunning to look at, her university resumé and her IQ nearly matched that of Ethan Skye. Eveline had hired the young woman as her main assistant to oversee all her businesses shortly after and had never once regretted her decision since.

"So?" Yuki asked as she came through the door with a steaming cup of coffee.

"So what?" Eveline muttered from where she sat behind her desk staring broodingly at the landscape outside the window.

A landscape she might not see for much longer.

Yuki rolled her eyes. "His name. What is it?"

Eveline frowned. "What makes you think there's a guy involved?"

Yuki leaned a hip against Eveline's desk. "'Cause the last time you looked this cranky, Rashid was still trying to get in your pants."

Eveline groaned as she recalled the gay sheikh who'd been the bane of her life last year. It was rare for her to accept clients since she'd become the boss of her own business. But when someone who was Arabian royalty offered to pay enough money to match her annual profits for the privilege of taking her out, Eveline could hardly say no.

The sheikh had turned out to be a handsome and incredibly charming man, so much so that Eveline had readily fallen into bed with him to find out if he would be as perfect a lover as he was a date. She'd been surprised to discover that he was gentle yet strangely reticent during sex. Eveline's instinctively knew the sheikh was hiding a secret. It was only after cajoling him into trying out some more daring stuff that she finally discovered what exactly pushed the man's buttons and made him go wild between the sheets.

The answer turned out to be asshole play and a strap on dildo.

"Well, it ain't Rashid," Eveline said. "The last time I heard from him, he was getting royally fucked by some Greek tycoon on a yacht in the Mediterranean and gave me a blow by blow of how many orgasms they'd achieved in one night."

Yuki blinked. "How many?"

Eveline sighed. "Twelve, apparently."

"Whoa," Yuki said, impressed. Her face brightened. "So, who's the new guy?"

Eveline rubbed a hand across her eyes. Yuki could be a dog with a bone when the mood struck her.

Well, I guess there's no harm in telling her. Besides, if Lincoln does make good on our agreement, she'll soon find out his identity anyway.

"At the moment, his name is 'Asshole'," Eveline said stiffly.

Yuki sucked air between her teeth. "Ouch. Is Asshole good in bed at least?"

"I wouldn't know," Eveline said darkly.

Yuki's eyes widened. "Wait. You mean you haven't done it yet and this guy's already got you in this state?!"

Eveline's frown deepened. "And what state would that be, exactly?"

A loud buzzing startled them then. Eveline stared at her cell phone where it vibrated on silent mode on the desk.

Yuki leaned over and studied the bright screen. Her eyebrows rose. "Someone called 'Asshole' is ringing you." She grinned at Eveline's scowl. "I can't wait to meet this guy. I bet he has a huge dick."

Eveline waited until her assistant left her office before picking up her cell. She took a deep breath, steeled herself, and tapped the answer button.

CHAPTER TEN

"Hello. You have reached the voice mail of Eveline Claude. If your name is Mr. Dickhead Asshole Hudson, please refrain from leaving a message and piss the hell right off."

Lincoln winced at Eveline's icy tone. He was relieved she'd picked up her cell despite her evident foul mood.

"Hi." A wave of tiredness washed over Lincoln as he toyed with the glass of scotch in his hand and looked out over Tokyo from where he stood in his penthouse lounge. "Look, I'm sorry I didn't call you earlier. My nephew got sick on Monday night. I flew over to Washington the morning I texted you."

Eveline drew a sharp breath at the other end of the line. "*What?!* Is he okay?!"

Lincoln swallowed and closed his eyes.

When his sister had called him at dawn four days ago and told him Lucas had been admitted to intensive care, Lincoln had feared the worst while he arranged for his jet to take him to the States. It turned out to be a nasty pneumonia that had been doing the rounds at the little boy's nursery and he made a rapid recovery after the antibiotics kicked in. He'd come out of intensive care after twenty-four hours and was now recovering at home.

"We all aged about ten years in the last few days, but yeah, he's alright," Lincoln said, his voice trembling slightly. He took a deep breath and cleared his throat. "He's a fighter."

Silence descended across the connection.

Lincoln tensed. "Eveline? You still there?"

"Yeah, I'm here," Eveline said with a heavy sigh. "Shit. I feel like a bitch now. Here I was calling you every name under the sun, and there you were, a doting uncle who flew halfway across the world to be with his nephew."

Lincoln grimaced. "I wanted to call but the time difference made it difficult. And I didn't want to text you."

"Why not?" Eveline said curiously.

Lincoln hesitated. "Because I wanted to hear your voice."

In the four days he'd been apart from Eveline, Lincoln had come to a shocking realization. One of things that had kept him strong while he comforted his sister and brother-in-law and supported them through the agonizing hours they'd spent in the hospital had been the memory of Eveline's face and voice. The way she arched her eyebrow. Her smile. Her sassy mouth. Her flashing eyes when she was angry. The way she'd flushed and moaned and cried out that night when she'd shattered in his arms before proceeding to deliver the best blow job he'd ever had straight after.

Lincoln had wanted to see her and experience all of it again so badly it'd taken everything he'd had not to get on his jet and come straight back to Tokyo the night Lucas got discharged from the hospital.

That was when Lincoln knew the woman had bewitched him. There was no other explanation for the irrational thoughts and desires that filled his every waking moment since he'd left her side.

Eveline's breath caught at the other end of the line at his upfront admission.

"Since you've been calling me names, I take it you've been thinking about me too?" Lincoln said quietly.

"You could say that," Eveline said huskily.

The memory of Eveline on her knees in front of him flashed before Lincoln's eyes at her throaty tone. His dick stirred. He twisted on his heels.

"Guess what I'm looking at right now?" he murmured.

DESPITE THE REMORSE REVERBERATING THROUGH HER, Eveline's nipples hardened at Lincoln's gravelly voice.

She felt like such a heel now that she knew where Lincoln had disappeared off to these past days. Something twisted in her chest at the thought of the pain he'd suffered. She knew how much Lincoln loved that little boy and she could tell from the way his voice had shaken a moment ago that he was still hurting to an extent.

"What—" Eveline cleared her suddenly croaky throat. "What are you looking at?"

"The couch," Lincoln said. "The one where we made out that night."

Heat flooded Eveline. She shifted in her chair, suddenly aroused.

"I can still taste you on my tongue," Lincoln murmured. "And smell your scent."

Eveline bit back a moan, a shiver of desire racing down her spine.

"And my fingers?" Lincoln said huskily. "Fuck, Eveline, my fingers are itching to touch you so badly. Both inside and out." He paused. "'Specially inside. And not just my fingers."

Eveline nearly lost her grip on her cell. "I—That's, er, nice!" she managed in a high-pitched squeak.

There was a short silence.

"Seriously?" Lincoln said. "After the way you screamed that night, you think it was just *nice*?"

Eveline groaned. She could tell from Lincoln's fake patronizing tone that he was teasing her again.

"Alright, it was fucking hot," she admitted grudgingly.

"Hmm. There *was* fucking involved, but it wasn't the kind of fucking I really had in mind when it comes to you. The next time I touch you, my dick will definitely be playing a primary role in our activities."

A familiar ache grew at the apex of Eveline's thighs at the memory of Lincoln's hands and his sizable junk.

He was right. She most definitely wanted more than just his fingers inside her.

"You free for drinks tonight?"

Eveline blinked. "Huh?"

Lincoln chuckled, clearly amused that he'd completely frazzled her brain with his teasing words. "I said, are you free for drinks tonight?"

Eveline cursed internally. "I could be."

"Is that a yes or a no, Eveline?" Lincoln said, his voice turning silky.

She shivered at the commanding undertone suddenly lacing his words.

"It's a yes," she breathed.

"Good. I'll pick you up at your place at eight?"

Eveline raised an eyebrow. "Sure. Where are we going?"

"It's a surprise," Lincoln said mysteriously.

CHAPTER ELEVEN

Eveline scowled. "Heads are gonna roll for this."

Lincoln grinned and handed her a cocktail glass. "Be nice. Barnaby can be very persuasive when he wants to be."

Lincoln turned and leaned his back against the bar as he took another good look at the place where he'd brought Eveline for the night.

Le Secret was set over four floors of a building straddling the corner of a popular intersection in Ginza. The main club area spanned a double-height first level and a circular mezzanine that overlooked a sunken section dominated by a sleek, rectangular bar. The interior was an eclectic blend of ultra-modern and vintage, with dazzling teardrop chandeliers and colorful Chesterfield arm chairs interspersed with top-of-the-line intelligent lighting and monochromatic high tables and bar stools. Although there were discreet areas scattered throughout the place, those who wanted a more intimate environment to enjoy the company of the elite escorts mingling with the crowd could have access to the private rooms and VIP lounges on the third and fourth floors if their membership allowed for it.

"I like it," Lincoln murmured. If the Tokyo branch of *Le Secret* was an indication of the rest of Eveline's clubs, then he could see why her business was so successful. "It's classy." He clinked his glass against Eveline's and stifled a smile at her mutinous expression. "Seriously, your assistant didn't know I was the 'Asshole' who'd gotten her boss all riled up these past few days."

Eveline grimaced before raising her glass in a toast. "Okay, even I have to admit that was below the belt."

Lincoln grinned and put out his hand. "Give me your cell."

Eveline narrowed her eyes. "Why?"

Lincoln raised an eyebrow haughtily. "I want to see whether you've changed my name or not."

Eveline grumbled something under her breath before slipping her phone out of her midnight blue clutch purse. She was wearing a matching wrap around dress with a plunging V neckline that exposed the creamy valley between her breasts, and a split up her left thigh that showed tantalizing glimpses of her bare, golden thigh. She'd completed the alluring look with open-toed, suede pumps that showcased her manicured, crimson nails and styled her hair so it swept across her right shoulder in soft, golden waves.

Though Lincoln would probably never admit it to Eveline, they'd almost not made it out of their building. One look at her when she'd opened the door to her condo had gotten him hard in a heartbeat.

Lincoln was grateful he'd asked Barnaby to book the private limo company on standby for his stay in Tokyo. It meant he'd had time to distract Eveline during their drive, so much so she hadn't realized they were outside her club's private rear entrance until she stepped out of the car.

The looks they'd been getting since they'd entered the main area told Lincoln Eveline's staff and the club's clients weren't used to seeing her with a date. He wasn't sure why, but that pleased him. A lot. Though Eveline was in the business of selling companionship, she was obviously more discriminate when it came to her own personal relationships.

Lincoln brought up Eveline's phone contacts and laughed when he saw the entry next to his name. "Lincoln Hudson, formerly 'Asshole'?"

"You're not out of the dog house yet," Eveline said tartly.

Lincoln crossed his ankles and leaned toward her slightly. "Oh yeah?"

The way Eveline's pupils dilated and her gaze dropped fleetingly to Lincoln's mouth told him his proximity was affecting her in all sorts of ways. His dick thickened at the thought of what he had planned for them tonight. One thing he was certain of: it was going to shock the hell out of Eveline, even more so than the fact that he'd brought her to her own club.

"Yeah," she said, her chest rising and falling just a

little bit faster. "We still haven't agreed the details of this—arrangement, yet."

Lincoln blinked. He'd almost forgotten why they were here in the first place. This was about the plot of land they were standing on right now.

"That's true," he said lightly. "We should remedy that." He looked at Eveline's phone and brought up the keyboard. "But first, let's change this."

"What are you doing?" Eveline said curiously. She angled her head and let out a bark of laughter when she saw what Lincoln had typed. "Lincoln 'Monster Meat' Hudson? *Seriously?!*"

Need slammed into Lincoln when Eveline's perfume swept over him. He slipped her cell inside her clutch purse and lowered his head to her left ear.

"Let's change location," he murmured.

Eveline shivered as Lincoln's hot breath caressed her skin.

He's driving me crazy!

She'd almost melted into a puddle of lust when she'd opened the door of her apartment earlier that evening and seen Lincoln dressed to the hilt in a formal black evening suit, crisp white shirt, and silk bow tie. The predatory look he'd given her as he scanned her from head to toe almost had her reaching for him and dragging him inside her condo and all the way up to her bedroom.

How they'd managed to make it to the limo and to

the club without ripping each other's clothes off was a miracle. For there was no mistaking the desire burning in Lincoln's eyes and the hungry way he'd been looking at her since he came to pick her up from her place.

Like he was right now.

"Okay," Eveline breathed.

She climbed off the bar stool and followed Lincoln as he headed up the stairs to the mezzanine. He navigated the crowded floor and guided her to the back, where a pair of private elevators led to the top floors of the building. Surprise flashed through Eveline when she saw the black and gold VIP card Lincoln slipped from his pocket. He smiled at her and pressed the access card against the security console.

"Wow, your secretary really has been busy," she muttered drily.

Lincoln's eyes sparkled with an enigmatic light as she joined him inside one of the elevators. She frowned when they stepped out on the fourth floor seconds later.

Where is he going?

Eveline's eyes widened when Lincoln turned and headed down the east corridor. He paused at the intersection at the end and took the passage on the right with the confidence of a man who knew exactly where he was going.

Eveline's pulse spiked when Lincoln stopped in front of the black, leather-padded, studded door at the far end of the hallway. Her steps faltered.

There's no way he knows what's inside—

Eveline tensed when Lincoln slipped the VIP card

in the security slot under the glittering, glass door knob.

Shit! Don't tell me Yuki gave his secretary THAT card!

A light-headed feeling swept over her when the lock clicked open.

"How the hell did you—," Eveline started hoarsely. She stopped and swallowed convulsively.

There were only two VIP cards that could access that room. One was in the safe in her office. The other was available to the highest echelon of the club membership and only after they signed a separate contract. Which meant Lincoln had paid in advance for full access to all *Le Secret*'s privileges.

Lincoln twisted the knob and pushed the door slightly ajar. Soft light spilled out from the other side. He turned and fixed Eveline with a heated stare before raising his hand palm up toward her.

"Come," he ordered.

Eveline shivered at Lincoln's commanding tone. She licked her suddenly dry lips. "Do you know what's in there?"

Lincoln's mouth curved in a sensual smile. "I do."

Eveline's knees turned to instant jelly at the torrid look in his eyes.

"And you're okay with that?!" she said, her knuckles whitening on her clutch purse.

Lincoln shrugged casually, as if what he was asking her to do right now was the most natural thing in the world. "I've had…some experience, yes."

Fuck.

Eveline couldn't believe this was happening. She hadn't gotten *that* vibe off Lincoln at all.

"Eveline," Lincoln said, his voice hardening slightly.

Eveline closed her eyes briefly and steeled herself before forcing her feet to move toward Lincoln. She took his hand and entered the VIP room ahead of him.

The very *special* VIP room.

CHAPTER TWELVE

Lincoln's heartbeat accelerated as he followed Eveline inside the room and closed the door, the click of the lock inordinately loud in the tense silence.

When Barnaby had given him the black and gold VIP card he'd managed to wrangle out of Eveline's assistant for the evening and told him about the unique space on the fourth floor, Lincoln's curiosity had been instantly aroused. He slipped the keycard in his jacket and studied the chamber they'd entered. A thrill rushed through him.

It had been the right decision to bring Eveline here.

Like the rest of *Le Secret*, the playroom was elegantly decorated in rich colors that highlighted its distinctive purpose and was equipped with top of the range luxury tools.

To the left was an orange spanking bench and a black mesh love swing tied to suspension bars. To the right, a beautiful green Victorian cast iron bathtub took pride position on the polished oak floor, next to a tall, leather-cushion padded restraining cross and a shelf stand carrying a variety of bottles, boxes, jars, and bath towels.

Oversized mirrors lined the soundproof, velvet-paneled walls and ceiling in strategic positions, most of them angled toward the playroom's showpiece.

Dominating the chamber was a raised platform. A king-size, black leather bondage bed with a purple studded headboard stood on it, the gold-colored metal restraints on the posts gleaming under the muted glow of the chandelier above it. Hanging off rows of stylish hooks on either side of the bed were a selection of metal, wood, leather, silk, and rope playthings designed for a Dom to restrain and stimulate a sub.

Lincoln hadn't lied to Eveline when he told her he had some experience with BDSM. Granted it'd been on the light side and he'd only been comfortable with the D/s part of that equation. The sexual partner who'd introduced him to it was an über-confident, A-list movie star with several awards to her name. The fact that she craved domination during sex had come as a surprise to Lincoln initially. Although it wasn't his usual kink, he'd enjoyed his time in the actress's playroom and had come away with a deeper understanding of what turned him on.

The only thing he'd been able to think of since he'd learned of the presence of a playroom in *Le Secret* was how fast he could get Eveline in it.

Lincoln's gaze settled on the back of Eveline's head where she stood motionless a few feet ahead of him, her clutch purse gripped tightly in her right hand. He glanced at a mirror ahead and to the right and caught sight of her reflection.

His breath locked in his throat. If what he was reading on Eveline's flushed face was correct, she was as turned on by this as he was. Lincoln knew he'd taken a heavy risk bringing Eveline here. This was pushing the boundaries of the agreement they'd come to a few days ago to its limits and he'd half expected her to refuse to even set foot in the room. She used to be a dominatrix after all, and he doubted she was used to being a submissive. The fact that she had agreed to do just that by taking his hand and entering the playroom sent a shiver of pure need down his spine.

Eveline Claude was truly unlike any woman he'd ever met before.

Lincoln's gaze shifted to the paperwork lying on the console table next to the door. He picked up the expensive black ballpoint pen atop it and signed the two contracts.

He'd already examined the documents when Eveline's assistant had forwarded copies to Barnaby that afternoon.

"Are those what I think they are?" Eveline said.

Lincoln looked up to find her facing him.

"Yes," he said, holding her gaze as he slowly put the pen down. "The first is for our original agreement. The second is for the use of this—," he glanced around, "—room."

Eveline tilted her head slightly to the side, a cool expression washing across her face. "So, does this mean I'm your escort tonight, Mr. Hudson?"

"No," Lincoln said.

Eveline blinked, surprise flashing in her eyes.

"I knew you would want something in writing," Lincoln continued. He stepped toward Eveline, took the clutch purse off her, and set it on the console table.

"Like I said, I would never pay you for sex, Eveline," he said quietly, his back to her. "I want whatever happens between us outside of dates and social occasions when I would like your company to be strictly personal." He paused before twisting slowly on his heels to look at her once more. "Is that okay with you?"

HOLY MOTHER OF GOD, I'M SO CLOSE TO COMING RIGHT now, all he has to do is touch me and I swear I'll go off like a fucking rocket!

If Eveline had been shocked by the fact that Lincoln knew about the playroom on the fourth floor of *Le Secret* and had paid the club's full annual premium fee in advance for the privilege of accessing it, she was utterly overwhelmed by what was going on between them right now.

She'd anticipated that Lincoln and she would have their first, full-on sexual encounter at either his place or hers. She knew it was going to be incredibly torrid, filthy, sweet, and probably the most deeply satisfying sex she would ever have. She was also confident Lincoln was not going to be an exclusive missionary position kind of guy. He'd clearly shown her that when he'd shamelessly finger fucked her on his couch a few nights ago.

That they were going to have penetrative sex for the first time here, in this room designed for the most decadent and wicked of human interactions, was so astounding and yet so breathtakingly electrifying she knew she was going to be a complete hot mess by the time he finished with her. And the light blazing in Lincoln's eyes told her he intended to keep them very busy indeed tonight.

Eveline realized Lincoln was waiting for her answer. She glanced at the contracts he'd signed, no longer surprised that he could so easily read her mind. He'd been right when he'd said she would want something in writing to secure the agreement they'd made that first night. Although the paperwork sitting on the console table now defined the clear boundaries of what was expected of both Lincoln and her for the duration of the engagement, Eveline knew they would both ignore them.

Their battle over the plot in Ginza was one thing. This, what was happening in this room right now, was another thing entirely.

Something like fear suddenly rushed through Eveline. She saw Lincoln stiffen and knew he'd picked up on the change in her mood.

"Evie?" he murmured, his husky voice laced with concern.

Eveline shuddered and closed her eyes at the diminutive of her name on Lincoln's lips. In that moment, she finally acknowledged the startling truth she'd been blind to these past days.

Lincoln Hudson had the power to break her. Not just financially, but emotionally and physically.

No one had ever made her want the things she wanted right now with this man she barely knew, this stranger who had entered her life less than a week ago.

To surrender herself fully to another person. To submit to his will. To give him all of who she was without expectation of receiving anything in return.

Eveline knew then that she was standing at a turning point in her life. She could either run from this or run toward it.

"Talk to me, Eveline," Lincoln said softly.

Footsteps rose ahead of her. Eveline felt Lincoln's body heat and smelled his heady, cologne-laced scent even before she opened her eyes and saw him standing in front of her.

He raised his hands and cradled her face gently. "Hey, if you don't want to do this, we can walk out of here right now."

Eveline took a shallow breath and narrowed her eyes. *I'm no quitter.*

With that thought in mind, she rose on her tip toes, raked her fingers through Lincoln's thick hair, and yanked his head down to kiss him.

CHAPTER THIRTEEN

LINCOLN GROANED AT THE FEEL OF EVELINE'S LIPS on his.

God, I've missed this!

He angled her face and plundered her mouth the way he'd been dying to do all evening, sucking and kissing her for long seconds before thrusting his tongue in the silky, sweet depths past her teeth to wrap around her own hot, wet flesh.

Eveline moaned and lowered her hands to his shoulders, her fingers clenching into his jacket. The sound she made sent a bolt of electricity straight to Lincoln's groin and reminded him why they were in this room right now.

He grabbed the back of her head, wrenched his mouth from hers, and held her jaw firmly in his grip, knowing she was ready for what was going to happen next.

"I didn't give you permission to kiss me now, did I, Eveline?" Lincoln growled.

Eveline's pupils flared at his dominating tone. She bit her lip, dropped her hands from his shoulders, and lowered herself back down on her heels, excitement bringing a rosy flush to her cheeks while she leveled her gaze at his chest.

For a second, Lincoln regretted his words. He desperately wanted Eveline to keep touching him.

This isn't about me. Tonight is all about her.

With that in mind, Lincoln let go of Eveline and slowly stepped behind her. He placed his hands on her shoulders and turned her so she faced a full-length mirror to the left.

"I think I need to punish you for your impudence, don't you, Eveline?"

Eveline's breathing accelerated as Lincoln trailed his fingers lazily down her arms, her chest rising and falling enticingly under his heated gaze. He reached the bow securing her dress at the left side of her waist and slipped the knot free. The dress fell open, the material catching on the curves of Eveline's full breasts.

Lincoln swallowed a groan of desire, his dick so hard he feared he was going to explode at any second. The only thing Eveline was wearing underneath was a little scrap of blue silk covering her sex.

He drew a shallow breath to calm his raging libido and hooked his index fingers in the edges of the dress where they rested atop her collarbones. Eveline shivered as he slowly peeled it off her shoulders and down her arms.

The material rustled and pooled on the floor at their feet.

Lincoln stepped back and devoured Eveline with his eyes where she stood naked before him but for her panties and her matching pumps.

Despite her slender shape, her muscles were beautifully formed and toned to perfection, the skin covering them golden and flawless. His gaze roamed the curve of her spine and the delicious globes of her ass before wandering down her long, mouthwatering thighs and calves. He looked up at the mirror facing them and perused her lush breasts and the stiff, pink nipples crowning them in the reflection, before running his eyes over the alluring dip of her waist and the flare of her hips.

A faint bruise on the outside of her left thigh drew his gaze.

Eveline's breath shuddered out of her when he skimmed a finger over it.

"What's this?" Lincoln murmured.

"Sandbag hit me when I wasn't paying attention," she said in a low voice, her gaze still not meeting his.

"Sandbag?" he repeated, puzzled.

"Kickboxing," Eveline replied.

Lincoln blinked. "You're a *kickboxer?!*"

Eveline looked at him then, fire flashing in her eyes briefly.

Lincoln shuddered. *Na-huh. We can't be having that.*

He reached around and gently pinched Eveline's right nipple between his thumb and forefinger.

She gasped and trembled, her thighs pressing together involuntarily. Lincoln's cock did press-ups against the zipper of his pants as he watched her squirm. He knew she was already wet down there.

"I said, are you a kickboxer, Eveline?" he hissed in her left ear as he rolled and tugged on her nipple.

"Yes," Eveline whispered in a shaky voice.

"Hmm. I'd like to see that one day," Lincoln said. He dipped his head and bit down on Eveline's earlobe. She trembled and arched her head to the side, offering him more access.

"But not tonight," Lincoln purred. He nipped at the sensitive skin on the side of her neck and was rewarded with a whimper. "Tonight, I want to see you on that bed." He took hold of her waist and turned her toward the platform in the middle of the room. "Climb on and lie on your back, Eveline."

Eveline licked her lips before stepping toward the bondage bed.

Lincoln undid his bow tie and left it hanging loose around his neck as he watched Eveline climb onto the leather mattress. She kept her shoes on and twisted around before lying on her back, her knees slightly raised and her arms spread out to her sides while she looked straight up.

Lincoln walked slowly around the bed, aware she was looking at their reflection in the ceiling mirror. She took a ragged breath and pressed her thighs together, clearly aroused by what she was seeing.

He dragged his gaze from the enticing view and inspected the tools hanging from the hooks on the wall. He selected a belt and a chain. His gaze lingering on a red ball gag for a moment. A shiver raced across his skin.

Although the idea was alluring, he wanted to hear every sound Eveline made when they were being intimate.

And make them she will.

He stepped onto the platform. "Put your hands above your head, Eveline."

Eveline obeyed instantly, her back arching slightly as she brought her arms up.

Lincoln secured her wrists with the belt, clipped the chain onto it, and fastened the end to a metal ring in the center of the headboard. He leaned back and inspected his handiwork. The chain had enough give for what he intended to do later. His gaze drifted from the metal links to the leather kissing Eveline's smooth skin and all the way down her sinfully seductive body to her sexy heels.

"Look at me," he ordered as he stared back up at her.

Eveline's gaze shifted to him.

Lincoln stilled at the expression in her eyes. Something twisted inside his chest.

He knew then that Eveline had never done this for another man before. Never played the role of a submissive. Never willingly surrendered her body and her pleasure to another.

That realization shook Lincoln to the core while he absorbed the mix of passion, vulnerability, and anticipation he could read in the electrifying blue depths of her gaze.

It took everything Lincoln had then not to untie Eveline, lift her in his arms, and take her back to his penthouse to make love to her in his bed. His breath shuddered out of him and his fingers clenched at his sides.

But he also wanted this. This power play of dominance and submission. Craved it. And he knew that even though Eveline wasn't used to it, she was hungering for the same thing just as badly.

Lincoln made a promise to himself then. He was going to treasure this moment and her.

CHAPTER FOURTEEN

EVELINE'S HEART STUTTERED WHEN SHE READ THE emotions dancing across Lincoln's face.

She could tell he'd hesitated a moment as he'd watched her naked, vulnerable form where he'd tied her to the bed. And she didn't think she'd mistaken the tenderness and possessiveness that had flashed in his darkening eyes.

Lincoln's expression grew determined once more.

"Do you want this, Eveline?" he said in a hard voice.

Eveline swallowed and dipped her chin slightly, the ache between her thighs a pulsing, hungry heat yearning for release. A release only Lincoln could give her.

"I asked you a question, Eveline," Lincoln said silkily.

Eveline shivered. "Yes."

"Yes, what?" Lincoln said.

"Yes, I want this," Eveline breathed.

"Show me," Lincoln ordered.

Eveline blinked. Lincoln narrowed his eyes, stepped to the wall, and took a riding crop down from a hook. Her belly clenched when he headed for the foot of the bed, climbed on the mattress, and loomed over her, his left hand coming to rest by her right ear.

"I said, show me, Eveline," he hissed.

Oh Jesus! He's going to make me—Eveline's passage spasmed with the faint wave of a distant orgasm—*fuck, come so hard in a minute!*

Eveline whimpered when Lincoln touched her left cheek with the riding crop. She spread her legs slightly, bent her knees, and rocked her hips up toward him, her heels digging into the bed.

Lincoln's eyes blazed with burning lust as he observed the wanton move. "Nice. Do that again."

Eveline's lips parted on shallow pants as she repeated the undulating motion, her gaze shifting briefly to the impressive erection denting Lincoln's dress pants.

Her attention arrowed in on his face when he moved the riding crop to her mouth. Blood pounded in her veins as he rubbed her lips sensuously with the smooth leather before nudging the end of the handle in between. Eveline fluttered her eyes closed at the wicked sensation of the round shaft entering her mouth. She wrapped her tongue around it and sucked, confident it was exactly what Lincoln wanted her to do.

The color on his cheeks when she opened her eyes and looked at him told Eveline she'd been right.

"I think you deserve a reward for that," he said gruffly.

There was a wet, popping sound when Lincoln removed the end of the whip from her mouth. He clenched his jaw and closed his eyes briefly.

Eveline bit back a smile, knowing he was as close to exploding as she was. Her amusement faded in a flash when he trailed the smooth, wet leather down her throat and onto her chest. Lincoln smiled faintly and held her thrilled gaze as he rubbed the end of the handle across her stiff right nipple.

"Oh!" Eveline gasped, her fingers biting into the belt binding her wrists.

"Like that?" Lincoln purred. He repeated the movement on her left nipple.

Eveline hummed with pleasure, the erotic friction of the wet leather on her sensitive flesh sending electricity shooting through her.

Lincoln bent down and replaced the riding crop with his fingers and mouth. Eveline moaned and whimpered as he tortured her breasts, each kiss, each suck, each pinch, each tug making her passage contract with a flood of heat. So lost was she in the pleasure Lincoln was giving her, Eveline didn't notice he'd slid the riding crop down her ribs and onto her quivering belly until he moved the leather tongue at the business end of the whip onto the mound of her sex. Eveline bit her lip as Lincoln pressed and rubbed it against her aroused folds.

"Hmm," Lincoln hummed around her left nipple. He let go with a wet, sucking noise that made her hips rock against the leather tongue and moved up to bring his mouth to her left ear. He nipped the earlobe with his teeth. "Is it me, or is the other end of this stick getting damp too?" he murmured as he continued stroking her intimately with the riding crop.

"*Fuck, Lincoln!*" Eveline hissed.

He stilled then and raised his head so he was looking down at her.

Eveline's heart flip-flopped when she stared into Lincoln's scorching gaze.

"Do you want me to fuck you, Eveline?" he said thickly.

Eveline had a sudden flashback to the conversation they'd had that first night at his penthouse.

Damn it, he'd been right all along!

"Yes," she said between gritted teeth. "I'm begging you!"

Lincoln's pupils flared. He watched her for a moment, the riding crop stilling on her flesh. "Why, I believe that does deserve the ultimate reward."

Eveline groaned when he rose and moved off the bed. He headed over to the shelf stand next to the restraining cross, removed a condom from a box, and returned to the bed. He dropped the foil on the mattress and grabbed her ankles. Eveline gasped when he pulled her toward him, the chain holding the leather belt around her wrists clanking as it extended.

Lincoln's breaths came in fast, harsh pants as he hooked the riding crop under her panties and peeled them down her thighs and her legs. He used his hands to drag the silky material over her feet, leaving her pumps on.

Eveline squirmed as Lincoln's molten gaze caressed her bare sex and the triangle of trimmed blond hair covering it.

"On second thought, I think we should hold off the fucking for a moment," he said feverishly.

Eveline gaped at him, so shocked she forgot she was supposed to be submitting to him.

"*What?!* Are you kidding me right now?!"

Lincoln chuckled then, evidently not minding one bit that they were no longer playing their little game. He closed his hands on Eveline's ankles and tugged her down the bed until her ass was on the edge of the mattress and her feet were dangling off.

"Foreplay's not over yet, Evie," Lincoln drawled, his face flushed with desire.

With that, he got on his knees, spread her thighs with his large hands, hooked her legs over his shoulders, and went down on her.

Eveline cried out at the wicked feel of Lincoln's mouth on the most intimate part of her body. Her belly clenched painfully, the waves of her orgasm dancing closer and closer.

He licked and sucked her folds, playing and teasing her for timeless seconds before parting them with his tongue and finding the very heart of her pleasure.

Eveline's breath froze as Lincoln closed his clever lips on her clit and sucked. A white haze filled her mind. She climaxed violently.

LINCOLN GRUNTED AND HELD ON FIRMLY TO EVELINE'S thighs as she writhed and rocked and rolled on the bed, her mouth open on incoherent cries, her heels digging into his back.

He let go of her swollen, sensitive clit and tongued her twitching opening as the pulses of her savage orgasm shuddered through her.

"Linc!" Eveline moaned, her voice hoarse with pleasure.

Lincoln shuddered at the diminutive, his cock so hard it was agony. He couldn't get enough of Eveline's heat. Her smell. Her taste. He knew he was close to coming just from pleasuring her with his mouth.

He groaned and carried on his sensual assault on her sex until he brought her to another screaming orgasm. Only then did Lincoln rise to his feet, unbuckle his belt, and slide his zipper down to free his straining cock.

Eveline's gaze burned as she watched him rip the condom open and sheath his trembling shaft with the lubed rubber, her cheeks and chest flushed from her recent climax.

"Untie me," she pleaded. "I want to touch you!"

Lincoln obliged and cast the belt and chain to the floor before returning to the foot of the bed. He grabbed Eveline's legs, hooked them around his waist, and guided his dick to the folds guarding her sex. He parted the swollen, pink lips and nudged the head of his shaft into her glistening opening.

Eveline cried out and reached up to grasp his corded arms.

Lincoln closed his hands on Eveline's hips and fixed her in position as he pushed into her ever so slowly, giving her passage time to adjust to his girth.

"Oh. My. God!" Eveline gasped, dropping her head back on the bed and arching her spine as he continued gliding in.

Lincoln cursed when Eveline clenched around his cock. He looked down to where he was entering her and groaned at the sight of his dick disappearing balls deep into her hot, tight passage.

He stilled and stared at Eveline, his heart hammering against his ribs. "You okay?"

Eveline looked at him dazedly, her breaths shuddering out of her in short, fast pants. She bit her lip and squeezed her inner muscles.

"Move! I'm begging you!" she groaned, fingers digging into his skin while she pressed her heels into his lower back.

Fuck.

Lincoln pulled his hips back and slammed them forward, thrusting his engorged, aching dick inside Eveline the way he'd been dying to do. She cried out, her back bowing beautifully off the bed. Lincoln gritted his teeth and set a slow, steady rhythm, fucking Eveline deep and hard.

She came on his sixth thrust, her insides contracting painfully on his sensitive flesh while she screamed in pleasure. Lincoln clenched his jaw and rolled his hips, his knuckles whitening on Eveline's skin while he drove his dick in and out of her convulsing passage, filling her trembling core over and over again.

The bed rocked as Lincoln gradually accelerated the pace of his thrusts, his body moving of its volition as it sought its release, harsh grunts leaving his throat every time he plunged his cock inside Eveline. Tension wound up his thighs and the base of his spine, the electric tingles of his orgasm gathering in slow waves until they became a hard, hot, tight ball in his lower belly and at the base of his dick.

Eveline sobbed out his name when she came again a moment later, tears leaking from her eyes where she'd squeezed them tightly shut, perspiration glistening on her face and chest.

Her convulsions finally tipped Lincoln over the edge. He stilled and let out an animal sound as his cock pulsed with the first savage wave of his climax.

Lincoln shuddered and leaned down over Eveline. He grabbed her hands where they gripped his arms, pinned them up by the side of her head, and linked his fingers with hers. He swooped and took her mouth in a fierce kiss as he pumped his throbbing, pulsating shaft into her.

Eveline's eyelids fluttered open. She gazed up at him, tears of ecstasy glittering on her lashes while her insides gripped and milked his cock with the pulses of her own intense orgasm, her tongue meeting his in an intimate dance that mimicked that of their lower bodies.

Blood roared in Lincoln when he finally stilled a

moment later. He bowed his head into the crook of Eveline's neck and rested his weight on her, his entire body trembling from his intense climax. She shuddered, her fingers clenching around his where their hands were still connected.

They panted loudly in the aftermath of their explosive coupling, their racing hearts thundering against one another.

"Wow," Eveline breathed.

Lincoln chuckled and lifted his head to look at her, his body still tingling from fading pulses of pleasure. "That good, huh?"

Eveline's lips curved slowly in a sated smile. "I don't normally cry during sex, so, *yeah*!"

Lincoln nuzzled her pert nose and dropped a kiss on her lips before slowly pulling out of her body. They both groaned when she involuntarily tightened around his thick length.

Eveline rose up on her elbows and watched as he stepped off the platform and discarded the used condom. He tucked his dick back in his pants and zipped up under her puzzled stare.

"Oh." She bit her lip, disappointment flashing in her eyes. "I thought there would be a round two."

Lincoln grinned, collected her panties and dress off the floor, and pulled her to her feet.

"The next rounds are going to be in my penthouse," he drawled.

"*Rounds?!* As in plural?" Eveline squealed, her delight obvious.

Lincoln laughed out loud and slapped her ass. "Yes. Now, get dressed."

CHAPTER FIFTEEN

"Should I be worried?" Lincoln said as Eveline headed down a dingy alleyway. "'Cause this looks like the kinda place where we might get mugged."

Eveline rolled her eyes and tugged on his hand. "Stop being a chicken and move those sexy legs of yours, Hudson."

Lincoln grinned as he headed into the balmy night with Eveline. They'd just shared a fantastic meal in Shinjuku; when Eveline told him she'd like to take him out for drinks at her favorite place in Tokyo, Lincoln thought they would be returning to *Le Secret* again.

It was a week since they'd visited the club's special VIP room. They'd gone back to his place that night and went on to have scorchingly hot and very loud sex in pretty much every room in the penthouse. Lincoln was thrilled to discover that Eveline had as strong a stamina as him in the bedroom and they'd met up at either his place or hers every night after that for some intense fucking sessions. In fact, they'd given each

107

other so many orgasms in the last week it was a miracle either of them could walk.

Eveline turned a corner and pulled Lincoln toward a discreet establishment fronted by steel doors and a row of roped stanchions guarded by a burly doorman.

The guy's face lit up when he spotted Eveline. "Miss Claude," he murmured with a smile as he unclipped the rope guarding the entrance. "It's great to see you."

"Hey, Kiba," Eveline said warmly. "Are the boys in tonight?"

"Yes," the doorman replied. "The whole gang's here."

Eveline giggled. "Oh wow. It's must be *hot* in there."

The doorman grinned. "If this was a rock concert, panties would be flying through the air right about now." He acknowledged Lincoln with a nod.

Lincoln dipped his chin at the doorman, curiosity and a flash of what felt a lot like jealousy bolting through him while he wondered who exactly Eveline's "boys" were. He glanced at the sign next to the steel doors before following Eveline inside the club. All it said was *Saron*.

Surprise filled Lincoln when they passed an elegant cloakroom. They navigated a tastefully decorated foyer and came to a short flight of wide, shallow steps leading to a sunken floor.

"Is this a gay club?" Lincoln said in Eveline's ear as they headed down the stairs.

Eveline grinned at him. "Yes. My friend owns it." She held on tightly to his hand and made a beeline for the bar.

Lincoln looked around. The place was packed with

men. Jazz music and a woman's sultry voice rose above the noise of conversation from the band playing under a spotlight on a raised podium at the far end. He studied the club and the patrons milling around them with rising interest.

Saron's decor was as unique and eclectic as *Le Secret*'s. It was evident from the looks of the clientele filling the place that it was as exclusive and upscale an establishment as Eveline's escort club. The crowd was thickest at the far end of the bar, where several men stood and sat drinking and talking at the polished mahogany counter, their backs to them.

Lincoln tensed slightly. From the avid glances the club patrons were casting at the small group, he knew instinctively that these were Eveline's "boys".

A striking blond bartender caught sight of Eveline as she approached with Lincoln at her side. His eyes sparkled and his face brightened with a stunning smile.

"Hey gorgeous," he said warmly.

"Hi handsome," Eveline replied. She let go of Lincoln's hand, leaned over the counter, and dropped a kiss on the bartender's cheek. He kissed her back.

Lincoln frowned at the over friendly exchange.

"Lincoln?" someone said in a stunned voice.

Lincoln turned and registered the man gaping at him from the left. "Gabe?!" He stared at the men beside Gabe as they looked around, surprise flashing through him. He recognized all of them.

Gabe Anderson, the design consultant who'd just completed one of the Hudson Group's most ambitious projects in the Pacific, stood at the bar next to Cameron

Sorvino, his lover and fiancé. Lounging on the barstools beside them were Rhys Damon and Wade Tucker, the brains behind Damon & Tucker, the design firm Gabe worked for and where he'd just made partner.

Eveline arched an eyebrow and looked curiously from Lincoln to the group of men while they called out warm greetings to one another and shook hands.

"You guys know each other?"

"Yeah," Lincoln said, relaxing. "Damon & Tucker have done several of my hotels and Gabe just finished my new place in Hawaii. The one where he and Cam are getting married."

Eveline blinked in surprise. "I didn't know that."

Gabe grimaced. "We're a bit late with the invites." He glanced at Cam. "Someone can't make up his mind about the card design."

"I told you I wanted silver," Cam said with a haughty sniff.

"And I say we go with white," Gabe said mutinously.

"Here we go again," Wade muttered with a groan. He turned to Rhys. "Hey, when we get married, you have carte blanche over the card design. In fact, you can arrange the entire thing to your heart's content."

Rhys's eyes glittered with a dangerous light. He took hold of Wade's tie and tightened the knot lovingly until Wade made a slight choking noise. "You're just saying that 'cause you don't want to help out, right?"

Wade grinned shamelessly. "Yup. You relish that sort of thing. I get hives just looking at flower arrangements."

Lincoln gazed at the two men, bemused. He hadn't realized they were an item too. He became conscious of a curious stare and looked around into the blond bartender's green eyes.

"Hey, Evie. Is this the guy?" the bartender said.

Lincoln narrowed his eyes as he observed the young man's teasing expression.

"It is," Eveline said. "And behave." She made the introductions. "Lincoln, this is Ethan Skye, the club owner's boyfriend. Ethan, Lincoln Hudson."

Ethan grinned. "I can see why you've been so…*busy* lately."

Eveline stuck her tongue out at him at the overt sexual innuendo.

Lincoln's unease faded. It was clear Eveline and the bartender enjoyed a close, sibling relationship.

Gabe studied Lincoln and Eveline with a curious stare. "Are you two, er—"

Eveline raised an eyebrow. "Dating? Kinda." She glanced at Lincoln.

They'd agreed not to disclose the details of their arrangement to anyone. As far as the world was concerned, they were seeing each other casually.

Movement to the right caught Lincoln's gaze. A tall man with brooding hazel eyes, dark hair, and a stubbled jaw joined them at the bar.

"Evie," the newcomer murmured. He stooped and dropped a kiss on Eveline's cheek.

Lincoln stiffened at the familiar way the man touched Eveline's shoulders.

"Hi, Joe," Eveline said warmly, oblivious to Lincoln's rising irritation.

The stranger looked around into Lincoln's faint frown. The amused expression in his eyes told Lincoln he knew exactly what he was thinking right now.

"And who's this?" the man drawled.

"That's the guy I was telling you about," Ethan said before Eveline could muster a reply. "You know, that night two weeks ago when you tied me up, spanked me, and had your hot, dirty, wicked way with me."

A bark of laughter escaped Eveline. Gabe groaned and put a hand over his eyes, his ears reddening.

"Jesus, Ethan. Time, place, and occasion," Cam muttered.

Rhys grinned while Wade shook his head with an expression that made it clear this kind of talk was a regular occurrence.

"Lincoln, this is Joe Cavendish, the owner of *Saron* and the filthy-mouthed blond over there," Eveline said.

Lincoln's shoulders loosened again. He shook hands with Joe, relieved. It was clear he had nothing to fear from Eveline's male friends.

That stray thought brought him up short. He blinked.

"Lincoln?" Eveline said.

Lincoln's pulse jumped at her puzzled expression.

Jeez. Since when has she been able to read me so well?

Lincoln forced a smile on his face to mask his unease at the unfamiliar emotion that had rushed through him. "It's nothing," he lied. He cocked an eyebrow and glanced from Joe to Ethan. "So, what does a man have to do to get a drink around here?"

A series of exclamations rose from the group at the bar.

"Now, that's a *loaded* question," Rhys ribbed.

"Yup," Wade said teasingly. "You may have to perform some *lip* service or two."

"Gotta be ready to *explore* your options, if you see what I mean?" Cam said.

Gabe groaned in embarrassment.

"You assholes," Eveline grumbled while Lincoln chuckled. "No one is going near this man's butt except me."

It was later that night, as they took a bath following two rounds of toe-curling sex during which Eveline marked his heinie with her teeth, that Lincoln finally asked her the question he'd been pondering for the last couple of days.

"So, there's this gig I have to go to next weekend. It's in Hawaii. Would you like to come with me?"

Eveline's fingers stilled where she was idly stroking his arms with her fingers. She tilted her head and looked up at him where she lay with her back against his chest in the water.

"Wow. An international date," she drawled. "It's been a while since I've been asked out on one of those." She grinned. "The last time, it was by an Arabian prince."

Lincoln's stomach twisted. This time, there was no denying the feeling that surged through him.

"Where did the prince take you?" he said in a light

tone, shoving the green-eyed monster smirking at him back down where it had come from.

"He hired a castle in France for the weekend," Eveline said. "It was fun. We went horseback riding, had some fantastic meals and," she shrugged, "you know."

Lincoln stiffened. Oh, his dick knew alright. What was bothering him more and more these days was that others knew too. Not that Eveline was seeing anyone else right now. Their agreement was exclusive and Lincoln knew Eveline wouldn't do anything to jeopardize it, considering what was at stake.

It was the fact that she would be free to sleep with any man when their business was over that was irritating the hell out of him. And Lincoln knew full well there was nothing he could do about it.

"Hmm." Eveline twisted in the bath and pushed up until she was straddling his hips and his stirring cock. She smiled and fondled his thickening length, her nipples hardening where her breasts stood exposed above the water. "So, what's the gig?"

Lincoln hissed and gripped her wrists under the water. "*Fuck*, that feels good." He opened his thighs to give Eveline better access and groaned when she reached down to fondle his balls while she stroked him. "It's a charity gig for *Médecins Sans Frontières*. It was my —," he faltered, his heart clenching with a spasm of sadness, "—mother's favorite charity when she was alive. My sister and I started fundraising for the organization after her death."

Eveline's hands stilled on his body. She studied him

for a moment before leaning forward and pressing a slow, soft kiss to his mouth.

"How did she die?" she murmured, her blue eyes glittering with compassion.

Lincoln hesitated. He never liked talking about his mother even at the best of times. Still, he knew Eveline would understand. And he realized he wanted her to know.

"It was a car accident," Lincoln admitted quietly. "It happened a month before my twenty-fifth birthday." He paused and grimaced. "I'm surprised you didn't read up on the gossip."

Eveline smiled faintly. "I've lived with enough rumors my whole life to know that they are full of shit." Her expression sobered. "I much prefer hearing the actual story from the horse's mouth."

Lincoln sighed. "It's a short one. Husband cheats religiously on wife throughout their marriage. Impregnates wife's best friend's daughter and forces her to have an abortion. Wife's best friend accuses wife of being a failure. Wife gets behind the wheel and—," his voice caught, "—crashes car. Son disavows father and leaves family home. The end."

Eveline sat back and stared at him with a thoughtful expression. "I'd say Son is pretty angry about it all still."

Lincoln frowned. "Wouldn't you be?"

Eveline kissed him again.

"Unlike you, I got to exercise my demons with a hockey stick," she said lightly. "Since beating your senator father to a pulp isn't the kind of man you are, I can see why this is eating at you."

Lincoln blinked, surprised and more than a little happy at the unexpected praise. He nipped at Eveline's lower lip with his teeth, curious. "And what kind of man am I, Eveline?"

Eveline's gaze grew hooded as she stared at him. "A good man." Her fingers grew busy on him once more. "A sexy man," she added when he grunted and dropped his forehead against hers, his breathing accelerating. "A man with the best dick my body has ever tasted," she whispered, moving down and rubbing her slick sex enticingly along his rock-hard length while she circled the sensitive head of his shaft with her thumb.

Lincoln swore, reached for a condom from the box he'd left on a ledge in the bathroom this past week for their shower sex sessions, and sheathed himself rapidly under the water. He took hold of Eveline's hips and positioned her over his dick before thrusting up.

Eveline moaned and dropped her head back, her fingers biting into his shoulders as he impaled her to the core in one smooth, hard glide, her passage clenching deliciously around his thick length.

Lincoln kissed and sucked Eveline's throat before turning his attention to her flushed breasts, the water sloshing around them while he fucked her slow and deep, her throaty cries and his harsh grunts echoing against the marble tiles.

CHAPTER SIXTEEN

Eveline accepted the glass of champagne Lincoln handed her and studied the crowd milling around the ballroom.

"This is an impressive turnout," she murmured. "Your sister's done a great job." She eyed Lincoln quizzically. "Isn't she supposed to be here already?"

"She texted to say she was running late," Lincoln replied.

His private jet had landed in Honolulu early that evening. The limo waiting on the tarmac had whisked them away to the hotel where the charity ball was being held, and they'd had time for a sumptuous meal in the Presidential suite he'd had Barnaby reserve for their overnight stay before they had to get ready for the event.

Lincoln caught the curious stares they were drawing and masked a smile. They'd only been in the room five minutes and they were already the center of attention. He was fully aware that this had more to do with the woman at his side than it did with his own reputation.

One look at Eveline when she'd stepped out of the bedroom fifteen minutes ago had had Lincoln so hot and hard he'd almost reached for his phone to tell his sister they weren't going to make the charity ball.

The gown Eveline had chosen to wear was an elegant, off the shoulder taffeta contraption, with a bodice that molded to her breasts like a second skin and highlighted her narrow waist and flaring hips. A split up the left side exposed one long bare leg and a crystal-studded, black stiletto Jimmy Choo sandal. She'd completed the seductive outfit with a diamond necklace, matching drop earrings, and a bracelet.

"Well, hello there, handsome," Eveline murmured as she stared at him from across the suite.

She strolled toward him, her gaze roaming his slicked back, gelled hair, the white tuxedo with the black, silk lapels and matching silk shirt hugging his large frame, his white bow-tie, and his gleaming, black dress shoes.

"I gotta say, Hudson, you dress up mighty fine," Eveline drawled, closing the distance between them. She stopped in front of him and ran a finger down the middle of his shirt, her touch leaving a scorching trail despite the presence of the material separating their skin. She paused when she reached the button holding his tux closed and tugged her lower lip between her teeth.

Lincoln swallowed when Eveline looked up at him with eyes that glittered with desire.

"I take it it would offend your sister immensely if we decided to ditch this gig and jump each other's bones instead?" Eveline said, hope lacing her husky voice.

Lincoln groaned and grasped her hand where she traced a sensuous pattern on his chest, not surprised in the slightest that they'd had the same thought. "Don't. I'm barely hanging in there as it is."

Eveline's gaze dropped to his groin. "Hmm. That looks... painful. You sure you don't want me to help you relieve that sizable—," she rose on her tip toes and carefully licked the pulse thrumming in his throat, "—ache before we leave?"

Lincoln's cock throbbed at the feel of Eveline's hot, wet flesh on his heated skin. He swore, grabbed her shoulders, and pushed her away slightly.

A throaty chuckle left Eveline's lips. Lincoln frowned at her teasing expression.

"I think that deserves payback," he said stiffly, adjusting his pants to hide his erection.

"Oh, I can take all the payback you can dish out, Linc," Eveline said tartly. "Just as long as you fuck me at some point in the next few hours."

They'd left their suite with Lincoln doing some quick calculations as to how long they would have to stay at the event before he could politely take his leave and fulfill Eveline's wish.

"Holy shit," someone said woodenly behind them.

Lincoln turned and blinked when a small figure barreled into his legs with a high-pitched shout of "Unka Leecon!" He grinned, handed his champagne glass to the woman who stood staring at them a couple of feet away, and hoisted the little boy hugging his legs up into his arms.

"Hi, Lucas," Lincoln said warmly, dropping a kiss on

the nose of the blond angel beaming at him. "You look very handsome tonight."

His nephew giggled and buried his face in Lincoln's throat, his chubby arms locking tightly around Lincoln's neck.

"Forget about my son," his sister Julia said in a deadpan voice, "the pair of you look fuck—," she stopped, her gaze straying briefly to the little boy in Lincoln's arms, "—hmm, hot. You two look hot." She smiled brightly at Eveline and offered her hand. "Hi, we haven't been introduced. I'm Julia, Lincoln's sister." She glanced at Lincoln with narrowed eyes. "Linc didn't tell me he was bringing a date."

Eveline smiled back and shook Julia's hand. "Eveline Claude. And he didn't. We are business associates."

Lincoln blinked, surprised.

"Here you are, honey." A man appeared through the crowd with two glasses of champagne. "Did you find —" Adam Goldman stopped and stared at Lincoln and Eveline.

Julia sighed and took one of the glasses off her husband. "I know, right." She frowned at him. "Babe, close your mouth. It's unbecoming to be ogling another woman when your wife is standing right here beside you." Julia sighed. "Eveline, this uncouth specimen of manhood here is my possibly-soon-to-be-ex husband, Adam. Adam, this is Eveline Claude, a business acquaintance of Lincoln's."

Eveline chuckled as the blond man flushed and dragged his shocked gaze from her and Lincoln.

"I'm not ogling," Adam told Julia in a stiff voice. "A State Deputy Attorney General does not ogle. It's just —," he looked apologetically from Lincoln to Eveline, "—well, you *do* make an attractive couple."

"Judging by the stares you two are getting, you're going to be the talk of the ball," Julia said drily.

"Yeah, well, I don't know how I feel about that," Lincoln muttered.

He was still taken aback that Eveline hadn't pretended they were dating to keep the fact that they were engaged in a business negotiation a secret.

Eveline leaned in closer. "This is your family," she murmured in Lincoln's ear while Julia and Adam engaged in a sarcastic exchange about her "soon-to-be-ex husband" reference. "I don't think we should lie to them."

Lincoln gazed at her steadily, a lighthearted feeling filling his chest at Eveline's words. He swallowed a curse when Lucas suddenly lunged out of his hold.

Eveline's eyes widened as the little boy practically climbed into her arms, her champagne sloshing slightly at the impact. She handed her glass to Lincoln and hoisted Lucas onto her waist, unheeding of her expensive dress.

Eveline eyed the little boy solemnly. "Hi there."

Lucas blushed and lowered his gaze. "Hi," he said shyly, burying his face in Eveline's neck.

Eveline grinned at Julia and Adam. "He's a sweetheart."

Lucas suddenly grabbed Eveline's shoulders, lifted himself up, and kissed her on the lips.

"Pretty lady," the little boy announced gravely in the shocked silence.

Eveline burst out laughing while Lincoln, Julia, and Adam gaped. "Wow, you guys start them young in your family," she said in between chuckles.

"I'm so sorry," Julia mumbled in a mortified voice. She took her son off Eveline and gave the little boy a stern look. "We don't go around kissing random women, Lucas."

The little boy blinked, his expression innocent. "But, pretty lady." He pointed at Eveline.

Eveline sniggered. Lincoln smiled and shook his head, not sure whether to be shocked or amused that his nephew was as captivated by the woman beside him as he had been the first time he'd met her.

"Well, this is a surprise," a woman murmured in a condescending tone behind him. "Harry and I weren't expecting to see you here tonight, Lincoln."

CHAPTER SEVENTEEN

Eveline saw Julia pale and felt Lincoln stiffen at her side.

She twisted on her heels and stared at the couple who'd appeared through the crowd. Recognition dawned. It was followed by a bolt of surprise.

A hush fell around them, the other guests turning into avid onlookers as they stared openly at their small group.

"Lincoln, Julia. It's lovely to see you," Senator Harry Hudson said in a reserved voice.

Eveline observed the senator thoughtfully as he released the arm of the silent woman beside him. She could see where Lincoln had inherited his hulking frame and charismatic looks from. She also knew she was looking at a version of Lincoln twenty years in the future. With one exception.

Lincoln had evidently inherited his mother's eyes, for the senator's were a cold, lifeless brown.

Harry Hudson walked across to Julia and pressed a light kiss to his daughter's cheek and his grandchild's head.

"Father," Julia murmured.

The senator dipped his chin at Adam before turning and stretching out a hand to Lincoln, his expression detached as he looked at his son.

Lincoln stared at his father as if he'd seen a ghost.

Eveline was aware Lincoln hadn't expected to see the senator tonight. From what he'd told her during the plane ride here, the senior Hudsons loved making an entrance and were notoriously late when it came to attending their social engagements. Lincoln had hoped to see his sister and leave the charity event before his father and stepmother showed up.

Eveline took a step toward Lincoln and slipped her hand onto the small of his back, silently encouraging him. Her heart twisted when she felt him shudder slightly beneath her touch. A hot feeling filled Eveline's chest as she gazed at Harry Hudson. In that moment, she hated the man who'd hurt Lincoln with a passion that stunned her.

Lincoln took a deep breath and reluctantly shook his father's hand. "Senator Hudson."

Eveline didn't miss the light that flashed deep in the senator's eyes at Lincoln's dispassionate tone. Harry Hudson was annoyed. She clenched her jaw.

Well, the bastard had better get used to it 'cause he's gonna be spitting mad in a minute.

"And who is this?" the senator said, his gaze moving smoothly to Eveline.

Eveline relaxed her shoulders, pasted the most charming smile she could muster on her face, and offered the senator her hand. "I'm Eveline Claude, a business associate of your son. It's nice to meet you, Senator."

The woman next to Harry Hudson blanched, her supercilious expression dissolving in an instant.

Eveline kept her gaze on the senator as he took her hand and leaned in to drop a gallant kiss on her cheek.

"I didn't know business associates were so... attractive these days," Harry Hudson murmured, his gaze lingering on Eveline's body for a beat. "What is it that you do—," he glanced at her unadorned ring finger, "—Miss Claude?"

Eveline masked the shudder of revulsion that rushed through her at the lascivious inflection in the senator's voice. She removed her hand from the older man's grip and slipped her fingers through Lincoln's where he stood rigidly at her side, his face dark with anger.

Eveline curved her lips into a full-blown, mega-watt grin that made the senator and several onlookers blink.

"Oh, I run an escort service," she stated breezily.

Lincoln's fingers twitched around Eveline's. Julia's jaw sagged while her husband's similarly dropped open at her side. Shocked gasps rose from the nearby onlookers. It was followed by a low murmur as word spread like wildfire through the ballroom.

Eveline saw Lincoln stare at her out of the corner of her eye. She squeezed his hand and looked squarely into the eyes of the pale woman beside Harry Hudson. "It's called *Le Secret*. You might have heard of it."

A wild-eyed look flashed on the face of the senator's second wife.

Gotcha.

Satisfaction coursed through Eveline as she stared at Nancy Hudson. It wasn't until that moment that she became one hundred percent certain where she knew the woman from.

Nancy Hudson regained her composure and glared challengingly at Eveline.

Eveline arched an eyebrow in return. Lincoln drew a sharp breath beside her. She turned her head and looked at him then, somewhat apprehensive. Relief flashed through her when she realized that his eyes were bereft of accusation or anger. Instead, he looked dazed and a little thrilled. She knew then that he'd guessed the truth she was silently trying to tell him.

Considering the binding confidentiality clause in the contracts of *Le Secret*'s clients, Eveline couldn't well come out and admit that Nancy Hudson was a regular customer at the New York branch of *Le Secret*. Or that the older woman had joined up under her alias and had a preference for men young enough to be her son.

"An escort service?" Harry Hudson said in a voice dripping with disdain. He stared from Eveline to his son, his dark eyes glittering with displeasure. "The company you keep could do with some improvement."

Rage shot through Eveline at the way the older man had spoken to Lincoln. She masked it behind another dazzling smile.

"Now, now, Harry, I said escort service, not brothel," she drawled. "I don't charge for sex."

A muffled giggle sounded from Eveline's right. She glanced at Julia and saw the woman turn slightly sideways, shoulders shaking and teeth biting into her lip to stop herself from laughing out loud. Her husband chewed the inside of his cheek behind her, his eyes similarly bright with mirth.

"In fact," Eveline added, her heart warming at Lincoln's sister and brother-in-law's response, "Linc and I are going into business together."

"Is that true?" Nancy Hudson asked in a shocked voice while her senator husband fumed silently at her side.

Lincoln's lips curved in an amused smile as he studied Eveline. "Yes, it is."

Eveline grinned. "Yup. We're thinking of putting a VIP escort club on the top floor of his new hotel in Tokyo. It's gonna have a revolving dance floor."

Lincoln cocked an eyebrow at her. "A *glass* revolving dance floor, wasn't it?"

Eveline nodded, warming to their game. "Uh-huh." She chewed her lower lip thoughtfully. "Although, that might be a bit cold for the strippers."

Lincoln grinned and lazily brought his champagne glass to his lips. "We'll just have to turn the heat up."

Eveline cocked her head to the side. "Oh, it's gonna be *hot* alright. But you do realize that means tassels, right?"

"Tassels?" he said in a puzzled voice before taking a sip of his drink.

"Nipple tassels," Eveline explained tartly. "For the topless barmen and waitresses," she added while Lincoln choked and spluttered on his drink and Julia snorted with tears in her eyes. "I was kinda counting on the cool temperature to keep things, you know, nice and perky."

Lincoln's bark of laughter echoed across the room.

A warm feeling surged inside Eveline at the uninhibited sound. She grinned, happily ignoring the angry stares of the senator and his wife, and the dumbfounded expressions of the people who'd overheard their conversation.

Oh, we're gonna be the talk of the ball, alright.

&a.

"I STILL CAN'T BELIEVE YOU DID THAT," LINCOLN chuckled.

Eveline looked up from where she was taking her shoes off. She grimaced. "Was it too much?"

Lincoln shook his head and held his hand out. Eveline twined her fingers through his and followed him as he headed onto the hotel's private beach.

An hour had passed since Lincoln had come face to face with his father in the hotel ballroom. The rage he'd felt at the time had long since faded, erased by the presence of the woman at his side and her bold admission.

More than the fact that Eveline wasn't afraid of standing up for herself and her business in a roomful of incredibly powerful people. More than the fact that she'd shown more grit than many of the men in Lincoln's circle as she faced down his father. More than the fact than Lincoln knew nearly every male under sixty in that ballroom would have killed to be in his shoes and at Eveline's side. Lincoln was grateful to her for one thing and one thing only: she'd made him forget that he was angry.

No one had ever done that before, not even his sister Julia.

"What are you thinking?" Eveline murmured as they strolled along the beach, their bare feet sinking in the soft, pale sand while surf crashed gently onto the shore to their right.

"I'm thinking that I can't believe my stepmother is a client of *Le Secret*," Lincoln muttered.

Eveline maintained a diplomatic silence.

Lincoln glanced at her curiously. "Were there other people in the ballroom? Men and women who are clients of *Le Secret*?"

Eveline flashed a grin at him. "My lips are sealed."

Lincoln chuckled.

The hotel noise and lights faded behind them. Soon, the only sounds were the swaying fronds of palm trees and the rhythmic lullaby of the ocean meeting land, and the only light that of the stars glittering like diamonds in the velvety darkness above them.

"This is nice," Eveline said quietly. She gazed up at the vast, shimmering sky, a dreamy expression on her face.

Lincoln slowed, his pulse suddenly racing as awareness slowly bloomed inside him.

Eveline paused up ahead and looked at him curiously over her shoulder when he stopped and tugged on her hand. "Linc? What's—"

Lincoln pulled Eveline close and swallowed the rest of her words with his mouth, his hands rising to cradle her face gently while he plundered her soft lips.

He knew why his heart was beating so fast. It wasn't desire that was filling his mind and body with heat and need.

He was falling in love with Eveline Claude.

No. Lincoln blinked as his soul finally told him what it had known for a while. *Too late.*

Eveline moaned below him, unaware of the staggering self-revelation resonating deep in his very marrow. She clutched his shoulders and rose on her toes to clash her tongue with his in a blistering mating dance, following where he led.

A different heat flooded Lincoln then. One that made his cock throb and harden with a hunger he knew only Eveline could assuage.

He tugged on the straps of Eveline's dress and freed her luscious breasts. A groan rumbled out of him as he dipped his head and closed his mouth on her left nipple. He licked and sucked the hard nub, his left hand dropping to fondle and play with her right one.

"Linc!" Eveline gasped.

Lincoln knew she was mindful of the fact that they were outside. He raised his head and glanced in the direction of the hotel.

"No one's going to come, Evie," he murmured, looking down at her. "It's just you, me, and the stars." He ran a finger lightly down her left cheek.

She stared at him, her face flushed and her eyes gleaming under the starlight. Lincoln swallowed a curse when his gaze dropped to her heaving chest and hard nipples.

Eveline took a step back, unzipped the gown, and wriggled out of it.

"Fuck, Evie," Lincoln said thickly, his rock-hard dick doing press-ups behind his zipper when he realized she'd gone commando under the dress.

"I've always wanted to have sex in the ocean," Eveline mumbled feverishly. She tugged her lower lip sexily between her teeth and started undressing him with a haste that made him chuckle.

By the time they were both naked, Lincoln's breaths were coming hard and fast too.

"Shit," Eveline said suddenly. Her gaze shifted from Lincoln's aroused shaft to his face, her expression falling comically. "Condom. We haven't got one."

Lincoln flashed a smile at her and leaned down to pick his dress pants. He removed a square foil from a pocket and waved it at Eveline. "Ta-da!"

Eveline laughed. "Oh my! I do love a man who's prepared for any eventuality."

Lincoln's pulse stuttered. He stilled. "Do you?" he said quietly.

Eveline's eyes grew hooded. She watched him for a silent moment. "I do," she finally said. "Here, let me."

She took the condom from Lincoln before he could

fully process the meaning behind her words, dropped to her knees, and kissed the sensitive head of his cock.

Lincoln hissed as Eveline slowly sheathed his trembling length with the rubber. He lifted her in his arms, carried her into the warm sea, and was inside her in under thirty seconds.

CHAPTER EIGHTEEN

Victor Kline grimaced and opened the file in front of him.

"The Hudson Group is willing to grant you a six-month lease for the plot in Ginza. We received this from Lincoln Hudson's secretary this morning. Hence why I called you in." The lawyer paused. "This can only mean that he wants you off his land afterward."

Eveline's heart thudded erratically in her chest as the lawyer removed a contract and slid it across the table. She picked it up with trembling hands and scanned the contents.

A week had passed since the charity ball in Hawaii. Although Eveline was painfully conscious Lincoln would soon be leaving Tokyo to return to New York and that they were nearing the end of the agreement they'd come to that first night at his penthouse, Lincoln had never broached the subject of what he intended to do with the plot in Ginza and they'd carried on seeing each other as normal.

Or fucking each other as normal.

Eveline gritted her teeth as she stared at the words printed on the paperwork in her hands.

Lincoln hadn't actually broken any promises. He'd done exactly what he'd said he would do. He'd enjoyed the services of an escort from *Le Secret* for a month, had never coerced her into having sex with him, and had made his final decision in a cold and professional manner.

Considering she could be just as ruthless in her business dealings, Eveline knew she shouldn't be surprised by the contract he'd had delivered to her lawyers.

Except she was. Not just surprised, but angry.

Lincoln Hudson had made her break every rule she'd ever set for herself when it came to her relationships with men. He'd smashed through her self-control, charmed her out of her panties, fucked her like she'd never been fucked before, and exposed every aspect of the real her to his probing eyes in the four weeks they'd been seeing each other. And after what had happened between them in Hawaii and the way he'd made love to her that night at the beach, Eveline thought Lincoln had also shown her the real him.

Because for one insane moment, it had sounded very much like Lincoln had asked her if she loved him.

It was only now, as pain slowly crushed her heart and numbed her body, that Eveline realized the answer she'd unconsciously given him under that star-filled sky was the truth.

She was in love with Lincoln. Had been in love with him probably since the night he took her to *Le Secret* and made love to her for the first time.

For once, Eveline truly believed she'd found a man who could be her match, both in and out of the bedroom. Someone who could infuriate her just as easily as he could make her laugh. Someone who could challenge her and make her feel things she's never felt before. Yearn for things she'd never wished for before. It looked like she'd been horribly wrong.

Her fingers clenched on the contract.

Lincoln had given her no inkling when she'd left his bed that morning that he'd already decided what to do about the plot in Ginza. The fact that he'd known how this would affect her and lied by deliberate omission made her sick to her stomach.

Shit, the guy deserves an Oscar for his performance.

"Eveline?"

Eveline startled and looked up at Kline.

He was watching her with a faint frown. "We still can still appeal this. And our case against the Nagatos is pretty strong. I think we stand an excellent chance of getting your money back from the original deal."

Eveline swallowed. For the first time in her life, she truly didn't care about the money.

"I—" She stopped, cleared the lump in her throat, and carefully slid the contract back to the lawyer. "Thanks, Victor. Can you or Malcolm keep me updated?"

"Sure," Kline murmured. His frown deepened as she rose to her feet and headed for the door. "Hey, are you okay?"

Eveline paused and looked at him over her shoulder. "Yes," she lied. "Why do you ask?"

"Because you look like you're about to cry," Kline said bluntly.

Eveline sniffed, straightened to her full height, and slipped her sunglasses down onto her nose. "It's just allergies."

She exited the conference room and headed briskly for the elevators. It wasn't until she'd walked through the rain pouring over Tokyo and reached her car that she realized her cheeks were wet for another reason entirely. She dropped her head against the steering wheel and muffled the sobs threatening to spill out of her before reaching for her cell, raindrops dripping off her hair and splashing onto the screen. She took a shuddering breath and hit a number on fast dial.

"Can I come over?" she mumbled when the call connected.

LINCOLN RANG EVELINE'S BUZZER. THOUGH HE COULD hear the faint sound of the rain and squall sweeping over Tokyo from the typhoon coming in off the Pacific, there was only silence from inside the condo. He waited a minute and pressed the buzzer again.

Eveline had told him she'd be home that night when she'd left his penthouse in the morning. He'd texted her late in the afternoon to tell her he was taking her out for dinner but never received a reply.

Which was a pity considering what he'd intended for them tonight. He'd had to make some last-minute arrangements in view of the weather, but it was still going to be pretty special.

A bout of nervousness darted through Lincoln at the thought of what he'd planned to say to Eveline that evening. He frowned faintly as he stared at the door and rang the buzzer one more time. There was no response.

Where is she?

Lincoln slipped his cell out of his pocket, brought up Eveline's number, and pressed the call button. His frown deepened when it failed to connect. He brought up another number and dialed it. Relief flashed through him when the second call went through.

"Yuki? This is Lincoln. I'm trying to get hold of Eveline. Is she still at *Le Secret*?"

Silence echoed across the connection.

Unease dawned inside Lincoln for the first time that evening. "Yuki?"

Yuki sighed at the other end of the line. "Well, this is awkward," she said coolly. "The answer to your question is no, Eveline isn't here right now."

Lincoln tensed at her tone. "What's wrong? And where is she?"

Yuki drew a sharp breath. "Seriously, you're asking me that? After what you did?" she said, her voice rising in disbelief.

Lincoln's mouth went dry. Something was very wrong.

"What the hell are you talking about, Yuki?" he said, his tone harsher than he'd intended.

Yuki muttered something rude under her breath. "Jeez, I know Eveline comes across as a cold, calculating bitch at times, but even she was surprised by that contract."

Lincoln's pulse stuttered. "What contract?" he mumbled between numb lips.

"The one Barnaby sent to Brooks & Kline this morning. About the Hudson Group granting *Le Secret* a six-month lease for the land in Ginza."

Blood roared in Lincoln's ears. "*Fuck!*" he whispered hoarsely after a shocked pause.

"Pretty sure that's what Eveline said too when she read the damn thing," Yuki said acerbically.

Lincoln's heart pounded like crazy as he stared blindly at Eveline's front door. "Look, can I put you on hold for a second?!"

"What do you mean, put me on hold? Hey, don't you dare—" Yuki's outraged voice disappeared as Lincoln brought up another number and stabbed the call button with his thumb.

"Well, hello there, Master," Barnaby said drily when the call connected.

"*Barnaby,*" Lincoln said between gritted teeth while he fought to control the storm of emotions raging through him, "*what did you send Eveline's lawyers this morning?*"

"I sent them the contract that was sitting in your

outbox," Barnaby said, his voice growing puzzled. "You know, the one you'd put today's date on for me to send."

"No, I didn't!" Lincoln snarled.

"Hmm, I'm pretty sure you did," Barnaby said. There was a pause. "I'm looking at it right now on my phone."

Lincoln put the call on speaker and brought up his mailbox. His legs went weak when he saw what Barnaby was clearly referring to.

"Fuck," Lincoln mumbled. "There was a second contract. I drafted it yesterday. And they weren't meant to go out until tomorrow. I got—," he swallowed and closed his eyes, fear twisting his heart, "—*shit!* I got the date wrong."

Barnaby was quiet for a moment. "That's not like you."

Lincoln leaned a hand on Eveline's front door and dropped his head against the wood, appalled at his own mistake. He knew very well the reason why he'd been so distracted this past week. And it had everything to do with the woman he had inadvertently hurt today.

She must be fucking furious, wherever she is right now!

"What was in the second contract?" Barnaby said curiously.

Lincoln drew a ragged breath. "It's the draft folder."

Barnaby's stunned voice came on the line a moment later. "You bought the freehold for the plot of land across the road from *Le Secret*?! And you're *sharing* it with Eveline?!"

Lincoln ran a hand through his hair. "It was meant

to be a surprise. I approached the owners and made them an offer they couldn't refuse. They agreed to sell it to me yesterday morning. I was—," he paused and inhaled shallowly, "—I was going to tell Eveline tonight, over dinner."

And not just about the land.

"It's not every day that I see the great Lincoln Hudson fuck up, but, er, you fucked up, man," Barnaby said bluntly. "Like, epically."

"Thanks," Lincoln groaned. "I've gotta to go. I have Yuki on hold on the other line." He disconnected and brought up Yuki's call, his pulse racing in his veins. "Yuki? There's been a misunderstanding. There was a second contract. Eveline was supposed to get both of them tomorrow, after I'd spoken to her about them tonight."

Icy silence resonated down the line.

"Really?" Yuki said in arctic voice. "And what, pray tell, was the second contract about? Because unless it involved ripping your heart out and giving it to her, I don't think—"

"I bought her the land across the road from *Le Secret,*" Lincoln said briskly. "I estimated it would take about six months to get the building ready for business if we have contractors working on it full time. The layout is similar to the one *Le Secret* is currently in."

Yuki gasped. "Fuck. Me."

Lincoln grimaced. "Sorry, but the only woman I'm intending to fuck for the rest of my life is Eveline. Now, where is she?"

CHAPTER NINETEEN

"I HOPE HIS DICK ROTS AND FALLS OFF!" EVELINE snarled. "In fact, I have a mind to find that asshole and kick him in the balls *right now!*"

She stopped, gripped her head with both hands, and let out an animal roar before pacing the polished wood floor once more, a litany of curses spilling past her lips.

Ethan leaned close to Joe. "I don't know what's scarier, the non-stop crying she did for the first six hours she was here, or the current episode of psychotic rage," he murmured in his lover's ear.

"I know." Joe frowned. "I've never seen her like this before."

Ethan chewed his lip as he watched Eveline stomp to and fro opposite where he and Joe sat on the couch in their lounge. He'd been surprised when he'd received Eveline's call earlier that day. Not only was it unlike Eveline to selfishly request that he drop everything and meet with her there and then, he'd also never heard her voice sound like that before. He'd called in another bartender to continue the prep at *Saron* and told Joe he was going home for the day.

One look at Eveline's puffy, red eyes and mascara-streaked face where she sat crying in front of the door to his and Joe's condo in her wet clothes had had Ethan ushering her into the apartment and into their shower. He'd given her a pair of his shorts and one of his shirts to change into before calling Joe to get his ass back to their place ASAP. It was clear that something had happened between Eveline and Lincoln. And it had taken several hours to get the truth out of Eveline.

Eveline stopped pacing and glared at Ethan and Joe.

"That's it!" she hissed, hands fisting at her sides. "No more men for me. They're all assholes!"

"Hey!" Ethan protested.

"Hush," Joe murmured drily out of the corner of his mouth. "She looks like she could physically hurt one of us right now."

Eveline narrowed her eyes. "Did you say something, Joe?"

"Nope," Joe lied, flashing a smile at her.

Eveline watched him suspiciously for a moment before stomping across the floor once more. "In fact, I think I'm gonna become a lesbian!" she declared. "Yup, no more dicks for me!"

Ethan swallowed a snort at this unlikely probability and arched an eyebrow at Joe while Eveline continued ranting across the way.

"So, tell me something. How come you took down

my stalker like it was nothing and you're scared of *her*?" he said in a low voice.

Joe looked at Ethan steadily. "I take it you've never seen Eveline in a fighting ring before?"

Ethan blinked, surprised. "You mean kickboxing? No, I haven't."

Joe sighed. "Thank your lucky stars. She's vicious when she gets riled up."

Ethan's cell buzzed in his jeans pocket. He fished it out and studied the number on the screen with a faint frown. He'd put the phone on silent a few hours ago.

"Who is it?" Joe said curiously.

"I don't know." Ethan took the call and brought the cell to his ear. "Hello?"

"Ethan?!"

Ethan's eyes widened. "Yuki? Sorry, I didn't recognize the num—"

"It's my private cell," Yuki interrupted excitedly. "Look, he's gonna be there any minute. Tell Eveline to turn her damn phone on. There's another contract in her mailbox!"

She disconnected. Ethan listened to the dial tone and looked to where Eveline had stopped in the middle of the lounge and stood staring at him.

"Hmm, Yuki says you should turn your phone on," he said.

Eveline scowled. "Why?"

The doorbell rang suddenly, startling them.

Ethan blinked. He had a sudden inkling about the identity of the person at their front door. The bell rang again and continued chiming as whoever was outside jammed the damn thing repeatedly with a finger.

Ethan kept a straight face while he stood up and started for the door. "Yuki said to check your mailbox for a second contract," he told Eveline over his shoulder.

"What?" Eveline snapped. "What the hell does that mean?"

Someone started pounding on the door. Joe frowned and rose to his feet as Ethan crossed the foyer.

Eveline grabbed her cell from a side table and switched it on. The phone buzzed violently in her hand as dozens of missed messages and call alerts came through.

Ethan turned the lock and opened the front door.

Lincoln stood on the threshold, face pale and fist raised to strike the panel again. He was soaking wet.

Ethan grimaced. "Wow. I'm not sure who looked more like a drowned rat, you or—"

"Where is she?" Lincoln said hoarsely, his eyes wild with desperation.

Ethan stood aside as Lincoln stormed past him and entered the condo, water dripping off his skin and clothes. An outraged cry erupted from the other side of the apartment.

&

EVELINE TOOK ONE LOOK AT LINCOLN WHERE HE'D slowed in the hallway and bolted toward him, rage distorting her vision. Joe swore and locked an arm around her waist when she dashed past him.

"Eveline, calm down!" he growled as she struggled in his hold. "Look, there's obviously more going on here than you think, so why don't you—"

Blood roared in Eveline's ears as her body reacted defensively. She gripped Joe above his left elbow, hooked her arm under his shoulder, lifted him in the air, and threw him to the ground in front of her.

Stunned silence descended around them in the wake of the harsh thud. Ethan gaped. Lincoln blanched.

"Ouch," Joe said with a wince where he lay on his back.

Eveline froze. Shock and remorse replaced her fury when she realized what she'd just done.

"I'm—*shit!* I'm sorry, Joe!" she mumbled as she dropped to her knees by his side. "Are you okay?!"

Joe sat up and grimaced as he rubbed the back of his head with his hand. "Yeah, I'm fine. The only thing that's hurt is my ego." He climbed to his feet and gave Eveline a stern look as she rose beside him. "Have you calmed down now?"

Eveline flushed and bit her lip before nodding meekly.

"Good," Joe said with a grunt. He glanced at Lincoln and the pool of water he was standing in. "Now, listen to the man before he floods our damn apartment."

Eveline stiffened. She steeled herself before turning toward Lincoln. She took a deep breath and met his gaze unflinchingly.

"What do you want?" she managed between gritted teeth.

Lincoln's knuckles whitened at his sides. He took a step toward her, his expression wary. "I'm sorry."

Eveline blinked, indignation a hot dagger twisting her belly. "*That's it?!* You've come all the way here to say—"

"I love you," Lincoln said quietly.

Eveline went deadly still. Her ears started buzzing with a distant ringing.

"There was a second contract," Lincoln continued as he took another step toward her. "You weren't meant to—"

"*What did you just say?*" Eveline whispered.

Lincoln finally came to a stop before her, his blue eyes glittering with such raw emotion Eveline's breath caught in her throat. This time, there was no mistaking the feeling blazing out of Lincoln.

"There's a second contract," Lincoln repeated. "The paperwork—"

"*No!*" Eveline said. She grabbed the front of his shirt and tugged him close, unheeding of the water soaking into her shirt. "Not that! What you said before!" Her voice broke and her vision blurred as fresh tears pooled in her eyes.

Lincoln folded her in his arms and tucked her head against his chest. "I love you," he whispered, his voice shaking. "I think I fell in love with you that day you stormed into my office and demanded I sell you the plot in Ginza. I just didn't know it at the—"

Eveline rose on her tip toes, looped her arms

around Lincoln's neck, and swallowed the rest of his words with her mouth. He cradled her face in his large hands and kissed her back just as heatedly, his face flushed and his body trembling against hers.

"Er," someone said in an awkward voice some time later.

CHAPTER TWENTY

Eveline blinked her eyes slowly open, desire a tempest threatening to sweep her away. She stared into Lincoln's glazed expression and saw him drowning in the same passion that filled her veins with fire.

He was also holding her up with her back against the wall and her legs wrapped around his waist, their bodies locked so tightly around each other it was a miracle they could even breathe.

Eveline looked over Lincoln's shoulder to where Ethan stood smiling goofily at them. He had his arms looped around Joe's waist while the latter covered his eyes with one hand, ears flushed with embarrassment.

"Not that we don't appreciate the peep show, but...," Ethan started.

Eveline slid out of Lincoln's hold, grabbed his hand, and headed across the condo and down a hallway to one of Ethan and Joe's guest bedrooms. She pushed Lincoln inside the room, turned, and closed the door in Ethan's face.

"Hey!" Ethan protested from the hallway. "You guys had better not get up to any hanky-panky in there!"

Eveline twisted on her heels and stared hotly at Lincoln, her back against the door.

"You were supposed to get both contracts tomorrow," Lincoln said, his expression contrite where he stood facing her. "I was going to take you out for dinner tonight and tell you about my proposal. I even booked the whole rooftop terrace of a hotel and hired a chef and a sommelier—"

"You have five minutes, Linc," Eveline said feverishly, her pulse racing as she forced herself to stay put. "After that, your clothes are coming off."

Lincoln's lips curved in a smile. "I bought the place opposite *Le Secret*. We'll share the freehold while you establish the club in the new building. Once my new hotel is up, I was going to suggest you either stay put or move *Le Secret* to the top of my building." His smile widened. "You know, like we talked about in Hawaii."

Eveline didn't realize she'd been holding her breath until she let out a ragged exhale. "That was just a joke," she mumbled.

"It was a good idea though," Lincoln said. "The club would have its own access at the side and you could run it independent of my hotel if you wanted to, although I think both our businesses would benefit from the collaboration."

The enormity of what Lincoln had done and was proposing finally sank into Eveline's consciousness. Her legs went weak.

Damn. He really does love me.

She inhaled shakily, pushed away from the door, and closed the distance between them. She stopped an inch from Lincoln and slowly ran her fingers up his wet tie.

"What if I don't want to be independent?" she murmured, tilting her head to the side while she slipped the knot free.

LINCOLN SWALLOWED AT THE DESIRE BURNING IN Eveline's eyes. The same desire that was threatening to consume him, body and soul.

"What if—," Eveline rose on her tip toes and brought her lips to Lincoln's right ear, "—I want to be tied down and taken any which way you want to take me?"

Fuck!

Lincoln's cock throbbed so hard he thought he was going to come there and then.

"I'm—," he paused and cleared his dry throat, "I'm okay with that, too."

Eveline stilled before lowering herself back down on her bare feet, her expression growing serious.

"There's only one problem," she said quietly. "You're leaving Tokyo."

Lincoln gently took her hands in his. "I'll have to go back to New York at some point, yes. But I can run my business from anywhere in the world. If Tokyo is where that's from in the future, then—"

Eveline grabbed the end of his tie, yanked his head

down, and kissed him hard. "You're crazy!" she said against his lips. "Why the hell would you make such a huge decision for your business based on—"

Lincoln took Eveline's mouth in a scorching kiss that had her melting against him.

"Because this—you—us," he murmured when he finally freed her lips. "It's more important to me than money."

Eveline shuddered in his arms. "God, Linc. You kill me," she whispered.

Lincoln shivered at the passion in her blue eyes. He bumped his forehead against hers.

"Say it, Evie." He took a ragged breath. "I need to hear the words."

Eveline swallowed before looping her arms around Lincoln's neck. "I love you, Lincoln 'Monster Meat' Hudson," she said solemnly, her gaze locked unblinkingly on his. "With all of my heart."

Lincoln's heart soared so high then he thought he would fly. He chuckled in the next instant.

Shit, only she could make me laugh when I'm this rock hard.

He arched an eyebrow at Eveline, barely holding on to his self-control. "Are the five minutes up?"

Eveline grinned. "Yup."

They were halfway through tearing each other's clothes off while they kissed each other hungrily when there was a knock at the door. They froze and stared at each other.

Lincoln strode bare chested and bare footed to the

door while Eveline yanked her shirt off the floor and held it in front of her.

Ethan stood on the threshold of the bedroom, a filthy grin on his face. He cast a box at Lincoln. "Here, condoms. The extra-large kind. Joe and I are gonna be at *Saron*. Let us know when you're, er, done." He looked over Lincoln's shoulder and winked at Eveline. "Have fun!"

Lincoln smiled as he watched Ethan saunter down the corridor to where Joe stood waiting for him, their jackets in hand. Eveline really did have great friends. He closed the bedroom door and twisted on his heels.

Eveline had dropped the shirt and stood facing him, stark naked and hands on her hips in a seductive pose that made all the blood in his body go instantly south.

"Let's test these bedsprings, shall we?" she said, her eyes burning bright as she cocked her head at the bed.

Lincoln stripped out of his wet pants and briefs as he stalked toward her, his dick pulsing with need. He cast the box of condoms on the bed, grabbed Eveline's butt, and lifted her up against him.

Eveline looped her arms around Lincoln's neck as their lips met in a blistering kiss, her legs locking automatically around his hips.

Lincoln growled when her damp, bare sex rubbed seductively against the back of his aching shaft. Her scent wrapped around him as he tumbled her backward onto the mattress. Although Lincoln wanted nothing more than to sink his cock so deep inside Eveline she'd see stars, he wanted to pleasure her first, to the point that she'd beg him to take her.

With that thought in mind, Lincoln pinned Eveline's hands above her head, lavished her breasts with kisses and bites while she twisted and panted beneath him, and worked his way slowly down her trembling body, his lips and tongue wrenching sultry moans from her throat.

Eveline shivered when Lincoln slipped a pillow under her ass, lifting her up slightly. He parted her thighs with his large hands, hooked her knees over his shoulders, and lowered his head to nuzzle her sex.

Lincoln looked up at Eveline and caught her feverish stare as she gazed down the length of her body at him, her knuckles whitening in the sheets above her head in anticipation of what was to come. This was the position the two of them had their most intense orgasms in.

Lincoln furrowed his tongue and licked Eveline's sex from bottom to top, parting her folds while he kept his eyes locked on hers. Her breath froze on her lips, pleasure dilating her pupils to black.

Lincoln's dick swelled and pulsated against the mattress at the velvety taste of Eveline and the knowledge that he would soon be buried in her heat. He suppressed his raging libido, gripped the inside of Eveline's thighs, and brought his full attention to driving her out of her mind as he circled and lapped at her clit with his tongue just the way he knew she liked it.

CHAPTER TWENTY-ONE

EVELINE CRIED OUT AND WRITHED ON THE BED AT THE pleasure Lincoln was giving her, her hips undulating and driving her sex greedily against his mouth while he worked her engorged flesh. He slipped two fingers inside her and hissed when she clenched tightly around him. He found the nub on the front wall of her vagina and rubbed it while he closed his lips on her clit and sucked deeply.

Sound and sight faded. Eveline was dimly aware of her body arching off the bed as she screamed and exploded in his arms. Lincoln nuzzled and lovingly kissed her sex as she convulsed from her powerful climax, her passage rhythmically squeezing and sucking at his fingers while he carried on working her G-spot.

By the time he brought her to her third orgasm, Eveline was sobbing his name, tears of ecstasy leaking from her eyes while sweat coated her flushed chest and belly in a fine sheen.

"Linc, please!" Eveline moaned.

Lincoln finally let go of his grip on her thighs and rose up on his knees, his body shuddering. He took a condom out of the box and ripped the foil with his teeth while he dropped his left hand to his leaking cock.

"Please what, Evie?" he growled as he rubbed himself, his blue eyes blazing with lust while he spread his pre-cum along his shaft.

Eveline tugged her lower lip between her teeth as she watched him roll the rubber over his inflamed dick. She wanted him inside her so bad she felt she would die if he didn't give her what she wanted in the next few seconds. She lifted her upper body off the bed, grabbed his corded forearms, and twined her legs around his waist.

"Please, enter me!" Eveline begged. *"Take me, Linc! Jesus, just fuck—"*

She screamed as Lincoln grasped her hips and gave her exactly what they both wanted, impaling her with his cock in a single thrust that had him balls deep inside her, her hungry passage stretching exquisitely to accommodate his girth.

However many times they'd had sex before, Eveline couldn't get enough of this feeling. This feeling of being filled to her very core.

Lincoln stilled above her and closed his eyes, the animal expression on his face telling her he was close to losing control. He unhooked her legs from around his waist, lifted them in the air, and dropped her ankles on his shoulders.

They both groaned as the move deepened the angle of Lincoln's penetration. Lincoln's breaths came in harsh, hard pants as he leaned over Eveline and grabbed her hands where she gripped the bedsheets, forcing her to bend her knees almost to her chest.

He looked down into her glazed eyes, pulled his hips back, and thrust back in, his dick pressing on her G-spot.

Eveline gasped, fiery tingles spreading through her body from where he was lodged deep inside her.

Lincoln repeated the move, slow and deep at first, then harder and faster, driving both of them higher and higher. The bed rocked and the springs squeaked, a sexy, filthy symphony to Eveline's rising cries and Lincoln's harsh grunts.

The first wave of Eveline's orgasm licked a blazing trail from the tips of her toes all the way up to her thighs. Her breath stuttered as the most incredible pressure pooled in her lower belly and arrowed in on her sex, tightening her entire body like a bow.

Lincoln's rigid shaft trembled inside her as he surfed the first wave of his own climax. He clenched his jaw and paused on the very cusp of their orgasms. Eveline looked up dazedly at him, her lashes wet with tears of pleasure. He leaned down and took her lips in a long, slow kiss.

Eveline's breath locked in her throat as she imprinted the moment in her mind forever. This was the first time they were truly making love and she wanted to remember every single second of it.

"I love you, Evie," Lincoln whispered against her mouth.

Eveline's heart overflowed with happiness at the reverent way Lincoln was looking at her, as if he too were fixing this moment in his memory.

"I love you, Linc," she whispered back huskily.

Lincoln drew back and slammed his cock home, finally delivering the climax they had desperately been reaching for. He swallowed her screams of pleasure as he thrust his pulsing shaft hard and deep inside her, her insides squeezing his dick so tight she never wanted to let go, her mind filled with a white haze of pure ecstasy.

It felt like hours before he finally moved her legs down to his hips and lowered his twitching body onto her. His heart raced like crazy against her chest as he shuddered and panted above her, her passage still spasming with aftershocks of pleasure around his cock where it remained buried inside her.

"I think that's a new record," Eveline said hoarsely.

Lincoln lifted his head from where he rested his face in the crook of her neck. He kissed the tip of her nose and licked the drop of sweat that fell from his face and onto her cheek. "Best fuck ever?"

Eveline shivered and smiled weakly. "Uh-huh."

"I aim to please," Lincoln said with chuckle.

They both moaned when the motion caused his dick to shift inside her. A loud groan rose above their breathy sounds. They froze and stared at each other.

"Hmm," Lincoln mumbled.

"What was that?" Eveline said tensely.

A series of creaks tore the air around them.

Lincoln closed his eyes and bit his lip, his face crunching up as he tried to stop himself from bursting out laughing. "I think that's the—"

The bed shuddered violently before collapsing beneath them in a cacophony of squeaks and splintering noises. The mattress landed on the wooden remains with a thud a second later, the two of them on top.

Silence filled the room when the last echo faded.

"*Tell me we didn't just break their bed?!*" Eveline said, horrified. "I was joking when I said we should test their bedsprings!"

Laughter finally rumbled up Lincoln's chest and erupted from his lips. He shook against Eveline, tears springing to his eyes.

"It's not funny, Linc," Eveline said in an admonishing voice. "Ethan and Joe had most of their stuff specially made and shipped in from Bali! This bed is unique!"

"Oh, it's unique, alright!" Lincoln chortled.

A giggle escaped Eveline. She straightened her face and gave him a stern look. "Mr. Hudson, behave!"

Lincoln rubbed his nose against hers. "I thought you specifically didn't want me to behave, Miss Claude?"

He thrust his hips lightly against her, his dick stirring deep inside her body. Eveline bit her lip and moaned.

Lincoln looked over his shoulder. "I reckon we should test that chair next," he said, tilting his head.

Eveline stared from him to the chair he'd indicated.

"I mean, we would be doing them a favor, right?" she said thoughtfully. "They should know if their expensive belongings can withstand the load, right?"

Lincoln chuckled, pulled out of Eveline, and sat up. He discarded the used condom before slipping a fresh one onto his erect cock.

"On second thought, your load is pretty heavy," Eveline said feverishly as she studied his dick.

Lincoln grinned, yanked her to her feet, and hoisted her up against his body. She coiled her arms and legs around him as he carried her over the remains of the bed and headed for the chair, her laughter mixing with his and echoing to the ceiling.

THE END

What happens when a business tycoon wakes up in the bed of her hot, devil assistant?

Get Hush (Nights #8)
Turn the page to read an extract now!

HUSH (NIGHTS SERIES BOOK 8) SPECIAL PREVIEW

CHAPTER ONE

LANA KEELE STIRRED AND SLOWLY BLINKED HER EYES
open. Searing light filled her vision. She winced and
twisted her head, a mumbled curse tumbling past her
lips. A wave of dizziness swept over her; her stomach
clenched painfully. Lana froze and swallowed the rush
of bile shooting up her throat. Hot daggers stabbed at
her temples. She moaned softly.

It was a moment before she realized she was lying
on her front on a bed. She stared blearily at the crisp
white pillow in her line of sight before rolling over
carefully onto her side. She studied the room she was
in with widening eyes.

Where the hell am I?

Cool gray linen kissed her skin. Her very much *bare*
skin.

Lana gasped and sat up. A shaky groan rumbled out
of her chest when the headache became a vise
squeezing her skull. She reached for the sheet wrapped

around her waist and legs and clutched it to her breasts.

She was only wearing her bra and panties.

What the hell happened last night?!

All Lana remembered was being in Shanghai's latest happening club and having drinks with the man she'd picked up at a bar while she'd been out with a girlfriend she hadn't seen since her college days. She dimly recalled drunkenly kissing the guy while her similarly inebriated friend hooked up with another man. The rest was a blur.

A door opened opposite the end of the bed. A man walked out of an en suite bathroom, his face obscured by the towel he was using to rub his hair dry.

Lana's pulse jumped. She stared up a pair of powerful, tanned legs, the mouth-watering deep V tantalizingly revealed at the top of the towel perched precariously on slim hips, a defined six-pack, a broad, muscular chest, and strong corded arms that bunched and flexed with the man's movements.

Holy crap, was the guy from the club this hot?!

The man paused and lowered the towel from his head. Lana felt the blood drain from her face.

No. Fucking. Way.

Tom Sutherland, her assistant and secretary of four years and the bane of her life, arched an eyebrow at her.

"Oh, you're up," he said in a matter-of-fact voice. "You'd better get dressed. You have an appointment in fifty minutes."

Lana's jaw sagged open as Tom walked over to a wardrobe and took down the neatly pressed suit, shirt, and tie draped on a clothes hanger hooked on the handle. Her eyes widened into saucers when she saw one of her work suits on an adjacent hanger, complete with a pair of matching panties and bra. Tom removed briefs from a chest of drawers and disappeared inside the bathroom.

Lana was still staring at the spot where he'd disappeared when he came out minutes later fully dressed. He sighed and glanced at his watch with a frown while he finished knotting his tie.

"Forty-five minutes, Lana," he said briskly. "Get your ass into gear."

Lana opened and closed her mouth soundlessly as he headed for the bedroom door.

"Hey! Wait a minute!" she spluttered. "Why am I in your bed, half naked?!"

Tom stopped and twisted on his heels, his hands in his pockets. Lana ignored the wild pounding of her heart as she watched the way the motion stretched the material of his shirt across his torso.

All it took was one look at his condescending expression for her to stiffen, the familiar irritation that plagued her whenever she was in his presence replacing the baffling feeling presently coursing through her.

There's no way in hell I just thought Tom Sutherland was attractive!

"Funny story," Tom said sardonically. "My boss

turned up on my doorstep at one in the morning, barged inside my apartment, stripped, and demanded sex." He cocked an eyebrow. "I felt I had to oblige her."

Panic slammed into Lana and sent her pulse into the stratosphere.

No. Dear God, please tell me we didn't—

Anger flashed through her when she detected the mocking light in Tom's eyes. "*You asshole!*" she hissed. "Tell me what really happened!"

Tom leaned against the doorjamb and crossed his ankles. Lana's gaze dropped to where his pants stretched across his strong thighs. She cursed internally and brought her eyes back up to his face, angry at herself for noticing his body once more.

This is Tom, for fuck's sake!

"The part about you turning up at an ungodly hour and entering my place without my permission is accurate, as was your demand for sex," Tom said coolly. "You then spent the next two hours throwing up in my bathroom. I sent your dress to the dry cleaners, put you to bed, and went to your penthouse to pick up a fresh change of clothes."

Lana glanced at the pillow next to the one she'd been lying on, her unspoken question hanging in the air.

Tom sighed. "I slept on the couch. Trust me, I wouldn't fuck you if you were the last woman on Earth."

Lana inhaled sharply as he turned and left the room. She scowled in the next instant.

"Oh yeah?! And I wouldn't sleep with you if you were the only asshole left alive on this entire planet!" she shouted after him, a familiar pain surging inside her chest.

Read Hush today

AFTERWORD

To all my friends who helped make this possible. You know who you are.

To you, my readers. Thank you for reading Eveline and Lincoln's story. I hope you loved this seventh book in the Nights series. I would be grateful if you could leave a review on Goodreads or on the store where you purchased this book. Reviews help readers like you find my books and I truly appreciate your honest opinions about my stories.

Make sure to sign up to my store newsletter for special deals on my books and new release alerts. Or you can sign up to my author newsletter instead to get upcoming release notifications, sneak peeks, and giveaways.

ABOUT THE AUTHOR

Ava Marie Salinger is the romance pen name of an Amazon bestselling author with a passion for writing addictive tales. Known for her action-packed and thrilling urban fantasy novels, she has expanded her repertoire with the introduction of the M/M urban fantasy romance series Fallen Messengers. Additionally, she has penned the scorching hot contemporary M/M romance series Nights and Twilight Falls as A.M. Salinger. When not immersed in her writing, Ava can be found curating inspiring music playlists, indulging in her love for nature, marveling at the latest gadgets, and savoring Chinese cuisine.

You can find all of Ava's books on her author store at shop.adstarrling.com